STEAMY
SWINGERS
Becoming a Shared Couple, Vol. 1

Martin & Jennie

JUST PLAIN BOB

WARNING

This book contains sexually explicit scenes and adult language. It may be considered offensive to some readers. This book is for sale to adults ONLY.

* * * * * * * * * * * * * * * * * * *

Please store your files wisely where they cannot be accessed by underage readers.

Please feel free to send me an email. Just know that these emails are filtered by my publisher. Good news is always welcome.

Just Plain Bob - **justplainbob@awesomeauthors.org**

About the Publisher

4Fun Publishing, a member of **BLVNP Incorporated**, 340 S. Lemon #6200, Walnut CA 91789, info@blvnp.com / legal@blvnp.com
NOTE: Due to the highly emotional reaction of some people to works of erotic fiction, any email sent to the above address that contains foul language or religious references is automatically deleted by our anti-spam software and will not be seen. All other communications are welcome.

DISCLAIMER

Becoming a Shared Couple, Vol. 1

Steamy Swingers

Martin and Jennie

By: Just Plain Bob

© Just Plain Bob 2015
ISBN: 978-1-68030-246-2

Chapter One

I sat on the edge of the bed and looked down at her napping and wondered about the way my life had changed. I got up and staggered into the bathroom and took a whiz surprised that she had left me enough strength to hold my dick and aim it. I washed my hands and as I dried them, I looked in the mirror. What I saw was a decent looking - not great - but decent looking man of thirty-five in reasonably good shape. By no means movie star quality and yet in the past six months I'd had more pussy than I could handle. And I didn't understand it; not even a little bit. I remembered the day it all started.

"Martin, could I see you in my office please?"

I got up and followed Bethany as she headed for her corner office. Following Beth was not a hard thing to do at all. Watching that tight butt move was an extremely enjoyable pastime. I followed her into her office and as she moved behind her desk, she asked me to close the door and then take a seat. As I closed the door, I wondered what Beth would want with me? She owned the company, but I had minimal contact with her as there was a VP and a regional manager between us and I couldn't help but wonder why she had skipped the chain of command and had come to me directly.

Beth looked at me across her desk, and it looked like she both wanted to say something and didn't want to say something. I just sat there and looked at her and waited. I saw the change of expression on her face and if I was reading it right, she had just decided to say:

"Fuck it; let's get this over with."

She took a deep breath and then said, "Martin, what I am going to say I want you to keep in the strictest confidence. It is going to sound weird, in fact, it is weird. But it is very important to me that this goes no farther than you. No one, and I do mean no one, should ever learn of our talk. Can I get you to promise me, without knowing what is going to be said, that you will keep this meeting and what is said to yourself?"

Like I would say no, right? In the first place I liked my job and Beth could just snap her fingers and I'd be gone, but there was also a curiosity about what was going on and if I said no I would never find out.

"Of course Mrs. Shaftner, I promise."

"You may call me Beth Martin. Is it Martin or would you prefer Marty?"

"Martin is what I usually answer to."

"Okay Martin, the first thing I need to tell you is that your job does not depend on the outcome of this meeting. You can say no and leave this office and go back to work without fear of any repercussions. No…, that isn't quite true and I guess that complete honesty is needed here. Your job may depend on your answer to what I'm going to ask you. That isn't a threat Martin as I hope you will understand by the time I am done.

"The company is in trouble Martin. We have lost several of our good accounts because of mishandling by Keith (my regional manager), and trying hard as I might, I haven't been able to get them back. Two of the accounts we lost, account for fifty percent of our billings. Quite frankly, Martin, I either need to get one of those two accounts back or I need to land another one just as big and I'm not having much luck at either. But one of the two has to happen or we will probably end up turning off the lights and locking the doors."

I sat there looking at her and wondering what any of that had to do with me. Oh, I understood that my job was toast if things didn't get turned around, but why did she have me in her office telling me this stuff?

"What do you know about the Montrose Corporation Martin?"

"I know that they are our largest account, but not much more than that."

"Well Martin, they are one of the accounts that we lost. Montrose is privately held and fifty-seven percent of the stock is owned by Angela Maybarry. Angela is married, has three grown children, is active in God only knows how many charitable organizations and she is a slut."

She saw the surprise on my face when she said that.

"It is true Martin; she is a slut and I know it for a fact. She is also a woman who likes power trips and who likes to play head games and right now she is playing one with me. I have talked with her several times over the last two weeks trying to win the account back and I finally got her to agree and resign with us, but only on one condition. It is a condition that I don't know that I can meet. Before I go any farther with this, I need you to answer my very personal question. What kind of shape is your marriage in?"

The truth was that my marriage sucked. Jennie and I had been married just short of six years and somewhere during the last three the spark had died. I loved her, but she was disinterested in me. She had let herself go to the point that when she did decide she wanted sex I had difficulty in getting it up for her. Not that our sex life was any great shakes before she lost interest; missionary position only, with the lights off and God help me if I said a word like cock, pussy, or ass. She was a good cook, kept a clean house and we didn't fight or argue so the marriage just coasted along.

"Why do you want to know about my marriage?"

"Because if it is a strong one I won't ask you to do what I would like you to do for me. I won't let myself be responsible for ruining anyone's marriage, not even to save the company. If you had a good marriage and did what I would be asking and your wife found out it could end your marriage."

"My marriage is only so-so. It could end tomorrow or next month or never. I don't know. What is this all about Beth?"

"It is about Angela's condition for bringing her business back to us. She wants you Martin. If you will spend a three day weekend with her, she will bring her account back to us."

"Me? She wants me? Why in God's name would she want me?"

"I told you Martin; the woman loves to play head games and fuck over people - excuse my French - and now she is playing with me. It could be that she wants to see how bad I want to save my business, how much I'm willing to crawl to do it. Maybe she just wanted to see if I had the guts to approach you and talk to you about it. Maybe she just wants to see me suffer, to show me that she has power over me. Or it could be that when she was here in the office Tuesday of last week and saw something about you that sparked an interest in her. I don't know. All I do know is that if you give her what she wants I'll get her account back and it will keep the doors open. What do you say Martin, can you help me out here?"

How in the hell can you answer something like that? But as soon as I had the thought I knew what the answer would be, what the answer had to be. My marriage wouldn't be a factor because even though I loved my wife the marriage itself wasn't much more than Jennie and I agreeing to co-exist. What was important to me was my job and if Beth was telling me the truth I stood to lose it. If I could save it by doing what Beth was asking it would be stupid of me not to do it. But I didn't want to go into it blind and I did have one concern.

"I've never seen Angela so to save us all some embarrassment I need to tell you a little something about me and my marriage."

I told Beth about Jennie and how I had trouble getting it up for her. "Depending on what this Angela looks like, I may or may not be able to get it up for her either."

"I don't expect that you will have a problem. A lot of men seem to find her rather sexy."

"The next thing I need to know is just what is meant by spending a long weekend together? Is this a situation where I'm supposed to be some sort of a servant? Is she into BD/SM and I'm going to have to be some kind of a slave for three days?"

"I've never heard that she is in any of that kind of stuff. She is a slut so I would expect that she will keep you sexually active for the weekend, but I could be wrong. Maybe all she wants is to rub my nose in the fact that she made me crawl and all she'll do is lounge around her pool with you and take you out for dinner and dancing. I honestly don't know. Can you do it?"

"Maybe. I don't know for sure, but I may be able to."

"Why the maybe?"

"I don't know that I can perform on demand. I've never been the kind of guy who could just whip it out and go. I have to work up to it; lots of foreplay and the like. You make it sound like I'm going to be a sex toy for the weekend and I'm just not sure I can do it performance wise."

"Well, she didn't put any conditions on what you would have to do. She just said she wanted you for the weekend. Give her the weekend and even if you don't - as you put it - perform, she still got her weekend and I met her condition."

Still, I hesitated to commit and Beth said, "Maybe I can give you some added incentive."

"What?"

"I've seen the way you look at me when I walk through the office and you've just told me about your almost non-existent sex life at home. Do this for me Martin and I promise you I'll keep your cock limp for the rest of your life."

"You serious?"

"Dead serious Martin. Save my company and I'll see to it that you never lack of sex again."

I jokingly said, "I don't suppose that you would put that in writing?"

Beth pulled a sheet of paper out of her desk drawer, wrote on it and then passed it over to me:

"I, Bethany Shaftner, promise Martin Beeman that if he assists me in getting the Montrose account for my company, I will be his sex toy until he gets tired of me."

And she had signed it!

"Do we have a deal?"

"Yes Beth, we do. I need Angela's phone number and her last name."

"I thought I gave it to you, but why would you need it?"

"I want to call her and set up a dinner date and since we haven't been introduced, I'll need to address her as Miss Whatever when I call and not Angela."

"It is Mrs., not Miss and her last name is Maybarry. Why are you going to call her for a dinner date?"

"Because standing on a street corner waiting for her to pick me up or knocking on a hotel room door and saying, "Hi, I'm Martin" just isn't my style. I'll ask her to dinner, we'll talk and then I'll follow her lead."

"You won't be sorry Martin, I promise you that," she said as she slid a piece of paper across the desk to me. "That's her cell phone number not her home phone number. Wouldn't want her husband to answer would we."

"She's married?"

"I thought I mentioned that."

"You did, but I guess I forgot it when you hit me with the rest of it."

"Yep, she's married; I did tell you she was a slut, didn't I?"

There is nothing in the world as daunting as a cold sales call and that is what the equivalent of my call to Mrs. Angela Maybarry would be. It would be awkward as hell for me, but at least we both knew what it was about. The phone rang five times before I heard a throaty:

"Hello?

"Mrs. Maybarry?"

"Yes?"

"My name is Martin Beeman and I'm calling to ask you to have dinner with me."

"Martin, how nice of you to call. I'd love to have dinner with you. When?"

"Well, I understand that you have, uh, other commitments? I guess the question would be what will work for you?"

"I do have something on for tonight; would tomorrow work for you?"

"Yes, it would. Where should I call for you?"

"Well, you did mention my other, how did you put it - commitments? I think we should just arrange to meet at the restaurant."

"Would Mario's work for you?"

"Yes, it would. They have a simply divine Veal Scaloppini. What time?"

"Say seven?"

"That will work just fine."

As I hung up the phone I made a mental note to ask Beth if I was on an expense account.

<<O>>

The next day I told Jennie that I had to work late and at six forty-five I was sitting at a table in Mario's sipping a vodka martini when I spotted an extremely good looking woman heading straight for me. I stood up and she extended a hand and said, "I'm Angela Maybarry" and I lied and said, "I know." I did the chair thing and then sat down opposite her and almost immediately a waitress was there and said:

"The usual Mrs. Maybarry?"

"Yes dear, and thank you for remembering."

As the waitress walked away Angela smiled at me and said, "This is a pleasant surprise. I didn't think the bitch had the guts to do it."

"I beg your pardon?"

"Oh don't act so surprised. I know she had to explain the situation to you. What did she promise you?"

"Nothing other than I could keep what I had."

"Keep what you had? I don't understand."

"It will keep the doors open which means I keep my job."

"She threatened to fire you if you didn't agree?"

"No, she just told me that if we didn't get your account back the company would go out of business and I'd be out looking for another job."

"And that's how she got you to agree?"

"No, what got me to agree was seeing you in the office last Tuesday."

"I didn't realize you even knew I was there."

"Well, I saw you" I lied, "And when she called me into her office and spelled out the deal I had to struggle not to look too eager. It wouldn't do to have her thinking I was such a pushover."

"Oh my, I didn't realize I'd picked a silver-tongued devil."

"Hardly, but that does bring up the question, why did you pick me?"

"Not to bruise your ego Martin, but the reason I picked you was that you were the only man there in the office that day."

"Aw shucks, and here I thought you looked at me and your heart started racing and it was all you could do to keep from coming over and throwing yourself at me."

"You don't know what is going on here, do you?"

"I haven't a clue."

"Since you are now a player in this little melodrama, I'll tell you what it is all about. Beth's parents and my parents were the best - and I do mean the best - of friends. They went everywhere together; weekends, vacations, didn't matter, they were always together and as a result, Beth and I grew up as close as sisters. I suppose you could say that until we reached twenty-one we were each other's best friend."

"What happened when you reached twenty-one?"

"She stole the man I intended to marry. She knew that I wanted him and was waiting for him to ask me to marry him, but she took him anyway. I'm glad she did because he turned out to be a cheating asshole, although I don't believe she knows it. He started cheating on her the week after they got back from their honeymoon. But even though I'm glad she took him away from me, I've never forgiven her for doing it. You just don't do something like that to your best friend. I promised myself someday I would get even with her."

"And that's what this is about?"

"Yes. My father gave her father a long term contract and he fully intended to renew its long term when it expired, but he passed on and left the business to me. When renewal time came, I didn't renew. She had to come begging to me, but that wasn't enough for me, so I came up with a way that I could humiliate her and here we are."

"So, the wild weekend I was planning on isn't really going to take place?"

"I didn't say that, now did I? No Martin, the weekend is on if you want it, and in fact I hope you do."

I sat there looking at that sexy good-looking woman and listening to her tell her story and I wanted more than anything to spend a long, hot weekend with her, but there was a problem. As long as it was a blackmail kind of situation, what Angela got out of the weekend didn't matter. But now that I had a choice, it has changed things.

"No matter what Beth still gets the account, right?"

"Yes Martin, she gets the account. I made her crawl and that is all I really wanted."

"Well then, I would really love to spend a long weekend with you, but I need to warn you that I might not be what you want."

"That's a first. I've never had a man try to back away from me before. How would you know what I might want?"

"Just a hunch. If a woman wants to spend a long weekend having hot sex, and that is the way that Beth put it to me, that you wanted me for a weekend of hot sex, she is going to expect hot sex and I'm just not sure that I can deliver and I wouldn't want to disappoint."

"Tell me more about this not being sure you can deliver. Just what are you expecting that I expect?"

"That's the problem, I don't know, but I do know me. I was a virgin when I married my wife and my wife was a virgin also. My only experience is with her and all she has ever allowed is sex in the missionary position. That is the extent of my sexual experience. Six years of sex in the missionary position and half of that with the lights off and her in a flannel nightgown pulled up to her waist."

"Oh, you poor dear," she said as she looked across the table at me. Then she smiled and said:

"All the more reason for us to have our weekend Martin. I can teach you so much. I'm getting wet just thinking about it. Are we on?"

Who am I to say no?

<<O>>

I told Jennie that I would be going on a weekend management retreat sponsored by the company and that I would return on Sunday night. I'm not even sure that she listened to me, but if she did, she didn't seem to care.

Angela suggested that we use her place since her husband would be out of town, but I told her I would be too nervous. I'd be constantly looking over my shoulder expecting him to come home early and catch us.

"Not to worry Martin, the asshole is with his girlfriend and no way is he going to leave her to hurry home to me."

"I'd still be nervous and I don't want anything to distract me."

She finally agreed and I checked us into the Hilton. Oh my God! I couldn't believe how much I had missed by limiting myself to what Jennie allowed me. Angela gave me my first blow job and then she taught me how to eat her pussy and after that it was just suck and fuck.

She sucked me off and swallowed my cum and then I ate her to an orgasm. She sucked me hard again and then had me do her doggie. That was followed by a sixty-nine, which was followed by more fucking. We did it cowgirl, reverse cowgirl, standing up and leaning against the wall, and we did it in the shower.

We went out for dinner on Saturday night and then went dancing. On the way back to the hotel, she took off her panties and handed them to the cab driver along with a fifty dollar bill and told him to cover the rear view mirror with her panties and pay attention to his driving. We fucked in the back seat as we drove across town. At the Hilton, we were alone in the elevator and she unzipped me and took my cock out and played with it all the way up to our floor.

Between our thrashing around on the bed, we talked - of all things - about Beth and her company. Angela wanted to know every little detail of the problems Beth was encountering and I told her what I could. I didn't' consider that I was being disloyal to Beth or the company by answering her questions because it was all information she could have gotten easily enough from other sources. I didn't think she was looking for information she could use against Beth and it turns out I was right. I told her the names of the other two substantial accounts that Beth had lost and she said that she knew the owners of both and then she asked me if I would like her help in trying to get them back and I told her I'd love it.

"I'll make some calls next week lover. But for now, we need to see if we can make some sweat. Come over here baby and let me have my lollipop."

It was the most exciting weekend of my life. As we were getting ready to check out on Sunday, I thanked her for the great time and the education. Then she said:

"You sound like you think it is over."

"I thought it was."

"Only if you want it to be Martin. I think we can have some good time together if you would like. Would you?"

"Very much so."

"Good. We can do some more on furthering your education."

"In what way?"

"We haven't done any anal yet baby, and there are still some positions we didn't get to. How about we get together Tuesday? Call me tomorrow around four and we can set it up."

"What about your husband?"

"What about him?"

"Won't he wonder at you being gone?"

"My husband and I have an unspoken agreement. He stays out of my way and he gets to continue living the easy life. If he causes me problems I'll throw his ass out."

"Doesn't sound like a great marriage at all."

"It isn't Martin. I caught him cheating on me and I forgave him and gave him a second chance, and one month later he cheated on me again and as far as I was concerned that ended the marriage."

"Why didn't you divorce him?"

"Because, financially, it is cheaper to keep the cheating asshole than to divorce him. One of the major disadvantages of having money Martin, is that other people want to take it away from you. A divorce would make the lawyers wealthy. Since I am the one with the money I would end up paying through the nose just to get rid of someone I ignore anyway. No baby, it is just cheaper to keep him."

As I drove home, I was thinking about how happy that weekend was going to make Jennie. She would never know why, but she would be happy that I never bothered her for sex again.

Beth was out of town on business when I went into work on Monday, but I did get a call from her around ten asking me how the weekend went. I told her that everything had gone well and she thanked me and told me that she would be back in town Thursday. Around eleven Angela called me and asked me if I could join her for lunch and I agreed to meet at Mario's again. When I got there she was sitting with another woman. I was introduced to Cathy Loring, the owner of Cartridge Incorporated and after a leisurely meal which was accompanied with a bottle of wine Angela told me that Cathy was a very good friend of hers and that Cathy knew about what I had done to get the Montrose account for Bev's company.

"Cathy is having some problems with her marriage Martin. She just discovered that her husband has been screwing his secretary and she wants a little revenge. If you would like to help her, she would be most appreciative. I'm sure you know that Cartridge is one of the accounts that Bev lost and there is a very good possibility that you could get the account back."

I try very hard not to be stupid so I immediately asked Cathy the most important question. "Would helping you get your revenge become public? Would you be throwing it in his face and telling him that I was the one who helped you hang the horns on him?"

"Of course not. It is interesting however that you mention throwing it into his face because that is very close to what I have planned for the bastard. If you help me, I'm going to go home and have him go down on me while I'm still fresh from being with you, so I guess you could say I'm going to put his face in it. How about it, you think you can help me?"

I turned to Angela and jokingly said, "I guess it is up to you. Are you willing to share me?"

Angela said, "Cathy can have you on the nights I can't take care of you."

"I'd be a fool not to say yes. When would you like to do it?"

Angela laughed and said, "We gambled on the probability that you would say yes, so we took a room at the Marriott. Would now be too soon?"

<<O>>

Friday morning around ten, Beth called me into her office and closed the door. The door no sooner closed behind me than she came to me, threw her arms around me, and then kissed me.

"She signed Martin, she signed and now I can breathe easy. Thank you Martin, thank you, thank you, thank you" and she kissed me again.

I thought Angela had drained me to the point where I wouldn't be able to get it up for at least another month. But Beth pressing herself as she kissed me, stirred me, and she felt me as I started to rise. She stepped back, looked at me, and then smiled.

"I did say you would never go without again, didn't I. Lock the door Martin. We wouldn't want to be interrupted, now would we?"

I turned and locked the door and when I turned back, she was stepping out of her panties. She dropped them in the middle of her desk and then walked over to me and turned her face up for a kiss. As our lips touched her tongue pushed into my mouth and I felt her hands unbuckling my belt. She broke the kiss and knelt in front of me and worked my trousers and briefs off of me, pushed them aside and then leaned forward, took my cock in her mouth and proceeded to give me magnificent head. In almost no time she had me ready to come and I told her so. Her hands clutched my butt cheeks and she pulled me into her mouth as deep as she was able and I let go. Her head kept bobbing as she swallowed and when I was spent she licked my cock like an ice cream cone for several seconds and then took me back into her mouth.

She worked on me until she got me hard again and then she stood up and walked over to her desk, bent herself at the waist and leaned on her elbows. She looked back over her shoulder at me, smiled at me and waited. As I slid my cock into her from behind I could not help but think about how my dry spell had ended. From almost no sex from Jennifer for years I suddenly had all I could handle - and I wondered how long I could make it last.

When it was over and I had my pants back on Beth had me sit down and tell her about my weekend. She wasn't interested in the sex part, just in anything that Angela might have said about Beth. I told her what Angela had said and she gave me a rueful smile.

"Oh, I know my husband cheats Martin. I'm well aware of what that asshole does. Did she also tell you that she fucked my husband a week after we returned from our honeymoon? That's how I know she is a slut Martin. The bitch seduced my husband before the ink was dry on the marriage license. Not that the asshole needed much in the way of seducing."

Her phone rang and she picked it up hello and listened for a minute and then she hung up. She stood up and said she had a meeting to go to and then she said:

"Thank you again Martin. I won't forget you, I promise."

"Before you go to your meeting I think you should read this" and I took the Cartridge Incorporated contract out of my pocket and gave it to her. "You need to check it over and make sure that I got the terms right and then call and confirm."

I gave her a smile and left her office.

And that is how it started. For the next eight months I had sex with Beth two or three times a week, sometimes in her office and sometimes in a hotel or motel when we took a long lunch. Once, she even took me home with her and I spent the night in her bed (after calling Jennie and telling her about the emergency business trip). Friday nights and every other weekend I spent with Angela. I occasionally got a call from Cathy, but not all that often. I had stopped even trying to make love to Jennie; she wasn't interested in me anyway and I was getting all I could handle from Beth, Angela, and Cathy.

Life was good.

Chapter Two

She stood at the sink looking out the window as she did the breakfast dishes. The yard looked, for lack of a better word, unkempt. The flower beds were full of color and the grass was green, but something was a little off. A little like a man dressed up in a suit and tie and with polished shoes that gleamed, but needing a haircut. Unkempt, needing a trim. Taking care of the yard had always been Martin's job, but he had been putting in so much time at work lately that he hadn't been able to keep up around the house.

She finished the dishes and headed for the living room. She dropped down on the couch, picked up the remote and started channel hopping and couldn't find anything that could keep her interest. She turned off the TV and got up to take a shower. The shower head had a bad washer or something and dripped. Just one more thing for Martin to take care of, one of these days. She washed and dried her hair and then toweled off. She reclined on the bed and picked up the latest issue of Redbook from the bedside stand and wondered why she kept renewing her subscription. She originally took out the subscription for household tips and recipes, but she hardly ever saw any of that anymore. Now it was all stuff like "Secrets for Lasting Love" and "Make the Ultimate Sex Connection" and "Sex Talk and Tips to Make Yourself More Alluring to Your Partner." You couldn't even get away from it when you did a simple thing like reading your horoscope.

Aquarius

January 20 - February 18

Focus on: Romance

The Sun and Saturn swing through your house of love through the 22nd. Put less energy into mundane matters and more into your love life. Your sex appeal will wow your partner - and awaken your self confidence.

What was with the constant attention to sex? Her issue of Cosmopolitan wasn't any better, in fact, if anything, it was worse. "How to Heat Up Sex." "The Touches He Will Beg for Again and Again."

"Beyond Kama Sutra - Eight sex positions you never thought of." Sex, sex, sex and more sex. God, didn't it ever stop? Sure, sex was nice every once in a while, but there was more to life than sex. It had taken her a long time to convince Martin of that, but he came around eventually. He didn't bug her now near as much as he used to. In fact, she could barely remember the last time he approached her.

She threw the magazine down and started thinking about the rest of her day. She had been invited to a pot-luck Tupperware party and she needed to come up with a dish to pass. Funny thing that. She wasn't a joiner, never had been, so what had prompted her to join the book discussion group at the library? That led to her making friends with Alice, Tina, and Marge. Those friendships led to her being invited to Avon and Tupperware get together parties, which gave her lots to do when Martin was away on business or working late. Tonight's party was going to be at Alice's house and she had never been there. She wondered if any of the girls liked to play cards. She could have a card party and invite them over as a way of saying thank you for inviting her to all of their get togethers. Salad! That's what she would make for the pot-luck, a nice five bean salad.

She had purchased some storage containers and a set of mixing bowls and had given her recipe for five bean salad to three other girls. The party had broken up and everyone had gone except Tina, Marge and Bev who she had just met. Alice had whispered to her to stick around when everyone else had gone.

"I've got something that you just have to see."

When everyone else had gone Alice led Tina, Marge, Bev and her down into the basement. The basement had been finished as a recreation room and there was a pool table at one end and a big screen TV at the other. Alice led them to the TV area and had them all sit down as she turned and put a tape in the VCR. The screen lit up and the words said, "Cierra Productions" present Angel Dust in "Lust at Home."

"Is this the one where she takes the guy with the eleven inch dick in her ass" Tina asked.

"No, that was "Lust in the Back Seat." This one is just out and you are not going to believe what she does in this one."

Jennie looked around the room at the eager expressions on the faces of the other women. She had never seen an X-rated video and she wasn't sure that she wanted to see one then, but getting up and leaving might cause a problem in her newfound relationship with the girls.

A sexy blonde with huge breasts appeared on the screen and all the other girls yelled out "Yeah!" They whistled and clapped, and when Alice saw the puzzlement on her face, she said:

"Her real name is Norma Speers and we went to school with her."

The plot, what little there was, seemed to be that the housewife was at home when the cable guy came. The housewife came onto him and screwed him and while they were doing it her husband's brother came in the house, saw what was going on and joined in. Jennie sat there amazed as she saw the woman take a penis in her mouth while one was in her vagina. She heard girls at school in the locker room talk about "giving head" but she could never picture it in her mind and when she heard about it she shivered in disgust. How could a woman do that? But the woman on the screen seemed to enjoy what she was doing. God knows the men were enjoying it.

On the screen the cable guy went to the phone and made a phone call. "I've got a hot one here," he said, "And I need some help" and he gave an address. Two more men showed up and Jennie's jaw dropped when the woman on the screen accepted a penis in her mouth, her anus and her vagina at the same time.

"What's so special about that? Hell, even I do that" Tina said.

"You do?" screamed Marge. "You slut you. You never told us you did threesomes and foursomes."

"That isn't what I meant. I've sucked off Bert and he's had my ass a lot."

"Oh that. We've probably all done that, I know I have" and Jennie saw Alice and Bev nod their heads in the affirmative.

"My God," she thought, "Am I the only normal person here?"

On the screen another man came in the door. "What the fuck!" he yelled, "What are you doing with my wife?"

"Hey man," said the cable guy, "She wanted it, so we are just helping her out."

"God damn. I didn't know I married a slut. Well fuck it, she's mine and I want her asshole."

"Okay man, it's yours" the cable guy said as he pulled out of the woman to make room for the husband. The husband moved up behind her and pushed his penis into the blonde's rectum and she screamed out: "Oh God, yes! Stuff me full of cock and fuck me!"

"Here comes the first one" Alice said as on the screen Angel Dust took a penis in each of her three orifices at the same time while she gave a hand job to the two men standing on either side of her.

"Isn't that wild?" Alice said. "Five at once. I may have to get real drunk some night so I can get loose enough to do something like that."

"Yeah, like you would" Marge said.

Alice said, "Hey, I might. I did two after the prom so I know I can do more than one."

"Yeah, but you were a cheerleading slut back then and not a wife and mother like you are now."

"I've still got what it takes. Every time I work out at the gym, I've got young studs looking at me and drooling."

Jennie had her eyes glued to the screen as the blonde and the men went through several different contortions. "Hey Jennie, are you okay" Tina asked.

Bev laughed and said, "Hell, she's just turned on. She wants to be where Norma is right now."

Jennie blushed, but she was also aware that what Bev had just said was true. She would never have believed it of herself, but she was turned on. Her panties were wet and while she didn't really want five men she did wish she was with Martin just then.

"Here comes the other hot part" Alice said, while on the screen, two men slid their members into Norma's vagina at the same time. "Yeah Norma," "You go girl" and "Go, go, go, go" rang through the room.

Everyone was gone and she was picking up what she had bought and was getting ready to leave, when Alice stopped her.

"Come on into the kitchen with me for a minute."

She followed Alice into the kitchen and Alice asked her to sit down for a second and when she did Alice opened a bottle of wine, poured two glasses and handed her one before sitting down at the table across from her.

"Did I do something wrong tonight" Alice asked.

"No. If you did, I don't know what it was."

"I looked over at you while we were watching Norma's tape and you looked like a deer caught in the headlights of an onrushing car. Haven't you ever seen a porn video before?"

"No, I never have."

"Did I embarrass you? If I did, I'm sorry."

"No, I wasn't so much embarrassed as I was shocked at seeing what she did."

"What bothered you? The oral? The anal?"

"All of it," she said and then she gulped down her wine. Alice refilled her glass and by the time the bottle was empty Alice knew Jennie's complete sexual history. "And you never had any desire to try any of it?"

"No, I didn't even know you could do some of it. I heard of oral sex when I was in high school, but I've never heard of anal."

"When you say you never tried oral, does that mean you have never had oral performed on you?"

"Oh God, no, not ever."

"Has your husband ever tried?"

"He did once, but after I screamed at him, he never tried again."

"Too bad sweetie, you have been missing a hell of a rush."

"Just a second" Alice said and she got up and left the room. When she came back, she had three video tapes in her hand and she handed them to her. "Here sweetie, look at these at your leisure time. If you are going to hang with us girls you need to know us for the perverts we are. None of us do this stuff, at least I don't think the others do, but we think about it and talk about it all the time. These will give you some insight into the way we talk and what we talk about after a couple of stiff ones. Drinks that is" she said as she giggled.

When she got home, for the first time in her married life, she wanted to make love so bad that she would have let Martin have her on the living room floor if he was there. But he wasn't there. He was out of town again on business.

<<O>>

The next day she watched the first of the videos Alice had given her. A beautiful redhead made love to four different men. In the first scene she took the man in her mouth and then in her vagina. In the second scene she did two men at the same time - one in her mouth and one in her vagina and in the next scene she sucked on a man and then let him put his penis into her rectum. The last scene she let three men use her at the same time. The thing that Jennie noticed was that the woman seemed to love everything she was doing.

How could a woman enjoy a penis in her mouth? How could she possibly like one pushed into her rectum? And then she had to ask herself why she was rubbing her vagina through her panties?

By the end of the week she had watched all three of the videos that Alice had given her and while she didn't understand it she had gotten excited every time she sat down and watched one and she had even masturbated a couple of times. She thought of Martin when she played with herself and wished his job didn't keep him away from home so much.

She returned the tapes to Alice when the book discussion group met at the library on the following Monday. After the meeting she had gone for coffee with Alice, Tina and Marge. The girls, by their actions and the way they behaved toward her, made it obvious that they considered her one of their group and not someone just sitting in, but was she really one of them? They were open about sex, they used words like cock, pussy, dick, cunt and ass and they discussed old and current boyfriends and their husbands. No subject seemed taboo to them. She wasn't like that. They were so full of life and outgoing and she was - face it - a stick in the mud compared to them. Why did they like her? What could they possibly see in her?

Over the next couple of weeks, she found herself spending more and more time with Alice, Tina, and Marge. She met other girls through them and became friends with Bev and a few others and she finally worked up enough nerve to invite them all to a card party at her house. The game that everybody seemed to know and like was double Pinochle and enough girls accepted to have two tables.

Martin was home that night and after he met the girls he went down into his basement workshop. Everyone seemed to have a good time and Tina said they should do it more often, maybe have a card party every other week, and the other girls seemed to like the idea. Martin came up as people were leaving and Alice asked him why he hadn't joined them.

"You already had eight players so I would have been the odd man out. Besides, my game is Euchre and not many people know it."

"Oh my God," Tina said, "Alice and I had given up hope of ever finding other Euchre players out here. Everyone played it back in Michigan, but no one out here seems to have even heard of it."

"You and Alice both play?"

"Yes, and we love it."

"Well, I play and Jennie is an absolute shark at the game. Maybe the next time the four of us can play."

"Screw the next time" Tina said, "I'm in no hurry to leave, how about right now?"

"I don't mind," Alice said as she looked from Jennie to Martin, "Ralph won't be home before midnight so I don't have to hurry home."

She looked at Martin and he must have seen that she wanted it. "Why not," he said as he started pulling out the extra cards to set up the deck. They cut for partners and Alice and Martin ended up teamed against Tina and Jennie. When the game broke up an hour later, they arranged to meet again on Thursday and talked about making it a weekly thing.

Jennie was not blind. She had seen the way that Tina and Alice had looked at Martin and she suddenly realized that it had been years since she had looked at him that way and that realization troubled her. Her epiphany came two weeks later. She was hosting another card party and they had just taken a break. She was in the basement getting a bag of ice out of the freezer. There was a heating vent just above the freezer. The floor above the freezer was the downstairs bathroom, when suddenly she heard a voice through the vent.

"Have you decided yet?"

"Yeah, I don't think I will. Jennie is a sweetheart and Lord does she ever have a beautiful face, but what she has let happen to her body is a crime." The voice was Bev's. "I think it would embarrass her if I invited her to a lingerie party. She obviously could never wear any of those things so I think it would be kinder of me not to ask her to come."

"Makes you wonder though."

"Wonder what?"

"How she keeps her husband looking like she does. God knows I'd let him put his shoes under my bed any day."

"He is rather good looking, isn't he."

She stood there holding the bag of ice cubes and thinking about what she'd just heard. Didn't want to embarrass her? Kinder not to invite her? They pitied Martin? Oh God, and she fought back the tears, got herself under control and went back up to the party.

When everyone was gone she locked herself in the bathroom, took off all of her clothes and then looked at herself in the mirror. She tried to imagine - no - she didn't need to try to imagine how Martin saw her, it was right there in front of her. No wonder he wasn't bothering to try and make love to her anymore. Good Lord, how had she ever let it get so bad.

The next morning when she woke up, she remembered the little magnet that her dad had put on the door of their refrigerator - "This is the first day of the rest of your life." Well, it was, and she was going to do something with the rest of that life. She showered, dressed, and then got out the yellow pages. Two hours later, she was a member of the Balance Fitness Center and a half hour after that, a trainer was showing her the equipment and how to use it. He set up a program for her to follow and then suggested that she might also consider looking into trying The South Beach Diet.

It was hard work and results didn't come overnight, but by the end of the month, she saw the change. Week after week, the change became more pronounced. Todd, the trainer she was working with, even made a 'soft' pass at her and it gave her hope that Martin would soon take notice of her again. She was starting to look good and feel good.

Her continued association with Alice and the other girls made some changes in her personality. She became a little more outgoing. In addition to the book discussion group she played cards with the girls every other week and every Wednesday was Euchre night with Martin, Alice, and Tina. When the girls talked about sex she joined in although she didn't have much to contribute. She was using words like cock and pussy and other words she would never have uttered six months ago.

The icing on the cake came the day Bev showed up for one of the card parties and said:

"Well look at you! Next time I have a lingerie party I can use you as a model."

Everyone noticed the change in her. Everyone commented on the change. Everyone but Martin. Had they grown so far apart that he didn't even notice her anymore? Well, at least he wasn't noticing anyone else. She saw the interest in the eyes of Tina, Marge, Alice and especially Bev, but Martin never seemed to notice that interest and he showed no signs of being interested in any of them other than as partners in Euchre.

It hurt! She had to admit it to herself - it hurt! All that hard work she had done and he hadn't noticed at all. It seemed that all he had time for anymore was his job. She was proud of her new look and yes, even of her new outlook on life and especially as that outlook pertained to sex. She was ready to give Martin her first blow job; she was ready to let him go down on her and yes, if he wanted it, she would bury her head in a pillow, stick her butt up in the air and let him have her ass.

But she also had her pride.

She had done all the work to make herself better for him, but she wasn't going to crawl to him and say, "Here. Look at me!" - he was going to have to notice her and come to her!

They rotated the bi-weekly card game and on that particular night the game was at Alice's house. When the game was over and people were leaving Alice stopped Marge, Tina, Bev and her and asked them to stick around. As soon as everyone else was gone Alice said:

"I've got Norma's newest. It's hot. Come on ladies, grab your wine glasses and let's go watch it."

The title, "Gang banging Housewife," staring Angel Dust scrolled across the screen and then the girls stomped and cheered and yelled out things like, "You go girl" as the sexy, busty blonde took on nine men in a fuck fest that lasted an hour and fifteen minutes. Angel

Dust took them two and three at a time and when one finished, he went and rested up and then came back again.

"Hard to believe that she was a tight assed prude in high school" Tina said.

"Damned hard to believe that she was a virgin when she left for California to become a star" said Marge.

"I guess even prudes can change" Alice said and she was looking at Jennie and smiling as she said it.

When everyone else was getting ready to go, Alice asked her to stay for a minute. When they were alone Alice said:

"Your face clouded over when I made my prude remark. What gives?"

Jennie had just enough wine in her to let it all come out and when she was done Alice said:

"Oh, you poor kid. I'm sorry and I'll talk to the other girls. We like Martin. He's a good looking guy and he's fun to flirt with and if he wasn't married to you a lot of the girls would probably be fighting to see who could land him, but none of us are going to try and steal your man. As far as the rest of it goes, I don't know. Maybe we need to give Martin a wake up call."

"How do I do that?"

"Let me think about it."

The next day Alice called her. "I thought about what we talked about last night and I think what we need is a girls' night out."

"A girls' night out? How will that make Martin notice me?"

"We salt the mine."

"We what?"

"It's what they did back during the gold rush days. If a man wanted to sell a low producing mine, he planted gold in the mine for the prospective buyers to find. It was called 'salting the mine.' What we will do is go out with the girls one night and the next morning when Martin walks into the kitchen he will find you cleaning out your purse. You will be taking several pieces of paper with phone numbers on them out of your purse and dropping them on the table in front of you. When he asks you what you are doing you tell him that guys kept hitting on you all night and giving you their phone numbers and you are just getting them out of your purse. If that doesn't make him stop and think and take a good look at you maybe you need to dump him and go find yourself a live wire."

The night she and Alice were going to put their plan into effect Martin called home and said he would be working late. She told him that she might not be home when he got there because she was going out with Alice and the girls for drinks. It was a blast! She, Alice, Tina, Marge and Bev had a table near the dance floor and five attractive, unescorted women were a magnet that pulled at every man in the place. There was a steady stream of men asking them to dance and offering to buy them drinks.

The plan Alice had of all the girls writing down a phone number on a slip of paper so the handwriting wouldn't look the same if Martin checked them, never got put into play. All of the girls got hit on so many times and so many phone numbers were pushed on them that fake numbers weren't needed.

Jennie had never had so much attention paid to her by so many different men in her life. The drinks were flowing and she was in a very good mood when she heard Bev say:

"I certainly wouldn't mind a taste of that."

"A taste of what?"

"That hunk sitting over there at the table by the hallway to the restrooms."

She looked over and saw Todd, the trainer she worked with at the gym, sitting with an older man and then she did something that was so out of character for her that she couldn't believe she did it.

"You want a taste of that? Well, since you are my friend I'll see if I can't get you that taste."

She got up and walked over to the table where Todd was sitting. He saw her coming so he stood up and greeted her with a brotherly hug. She cut right to it.

"I need a favor."

"If it is something I can do, you've got it."

"See that gorgeous redhead at that table over there" and she pointed to where Bev was sitting, "She has been sitting there and staring at you and I decided to try my hand at match making. Do me a favor and ask her for a dance."

Todd turned to the man he was sitting with and asked, "Would you mind if I abandoned you?"

"Not at all, but I think it's only fair that if she takes you away from me she should have to stay and keep me company."

Todd looked at her and raised an eyebrow. She smiled and said, "I guess I can make that sacrifice for Bev" and she sat down on the seat that Todd had just vacated and extended her hand as she said, "I'm Jennie."

The man took her hand and as he said, "Hi Jennie, I'm Frank" she felt a spark. Something about the man appealed to her and the thought caused her to shiver. She looked over and saw Todd walking Bev out onto the dance floor and Frank asked her if she would like to dance. Given the strange feeling she was having she decided that maybe it would be best to get away from the table where they were alone and get out there on the crowded dance floor where there were a lot of people around.

Bad move she realized as they got out on the floor. It was crowded enough that she and Frank were pushed together and as he took her in his arms, she felt her body tingle and that wasn't all she felt. He was hard and it was pressing into her. What made it worse was that he looked a little like one of the actors she had seen on one of Alice's porn tapes. The thought of that tape and what she had done while she was watching it and now dancing with a man who looked like... Oh God, what was she thinking? Why was her entire body tingling and why were her panties getting damp?

The dance turned into three and then he took her back to his table. Several drinks and several dances later she noticed that the other girls were gone, including Alice who was her ride. She excused herself and checked all the bathrooms, but couldn't find Alice. When she returned to the table Frank asked:

"Something wrong?"

"My ride is gone."

"No problem" Frank said, "I'll see to it that you get home. One more drink and we'll dance the rest of this set and I'll run you home."

It was three more drinks before they left the bar. She felt... well, she didn't really know how she felt. She was turned on from all the close dancing, she had done with Frank, and from having his cock rubbed against her so much. She was pleased to know that she had turned him on - knowing that she was sexually alluring.

She was uncomfortable being in a car with a strange man (well, even though they had danced for hours she didn't really know him) but at the same time she was excited. He wanted her and it had been a long time since she had felt wanted. There was something about him, some sort of animal or sexual magnetism that had caused the spark when she first met him.

The drinks had her feeling really good and upbeat and all the confusing thoughts were rolling around in her head so she really wasn't prepared for it when Frank slid across the car seat, took her in his arms and kissed her. His tongue teased her lips and she shivered as she opened her mouth to let it in. The drinks, the excitement she felt and it having been so long since she'd last had any affection at all combined in that one moment and caused any idea of resistance to fade. She eagerly returned Frank's kiss, sending her own tongue searching. She didn't even notice when he got his hands up under her blouse and unsnapped her brassiere. It wasn't until she felt one of her nipples being rolled between a thumb and forefinger that she was aware of how far he had gotten.

Little electric shocks were flowing through her body directly to her pussy, and she spread her legs, which Frank took as an open invitation, soon his fingers sought out her treasure. When his fingers entered her, she moaned and Frank broke his kiss long enough to murmur;

"Cars are for teenagers, but you are so hot that I just can't pass up this opportunity."

He kissed her again and as their tongues played, he unzipped himself and pulled out his erection. He took her right hand and put it on his erect cock and she grasped it and started stroking it. Suddenly, that hot tube of flesh reminded her that she was a married woman, that she loved her husband and what she was doing was wrong. She let go of Frank's cock and he sensed that things were about to change. But before she could do anything, he pushed her back on the seat, pushed the gusset of her panties aside and pushed his cock into her cunt.

She felt the cock drive into her and even though she knew it was wrong, it still felt good. All the protests, she was going to make, were forgotten as Frank drove deep into her and started fucking her. "Oh God Martin, I'm so sorry" flashed through her mind as she gave herself up to Frank. Her arms went around him and she pulled her knees back to open herself to him and all thoughts of Martin disappeared.

Cars may have been for teenagers, but then the two of them fucked like teenagers. Frank came in her and as he pulled out, she whined at being left hanging so he got her into the back seat and fucked her some more. They did some serious necking and then Frank fucked her for the third time. When it was over she told him that she needed to get home before her husband got worried. Frank stopped a block from her house and they kissed goodnight. When they pulled into her driveway and she was about to get out of the car Frank said:

"I'll call you."

She only hesitated a moment before saying, "I'd like that" and then she went into the house worried about how she would be able to face Martin. It was a wasted worry as he was in bed sound asleep. She crawled in next to him and then she lay there staring up at the ceiling. A tear trickled down her cheek at the thought that she had betrayed her husband and she didn't even know why. Not only that, but she had left the door open to do it again. Why had she told Frank that she would like him to call her? She didn't want Frank, she wanted Martin.

The phone rang as she was fixing Martin's breakfast. She answered it and it was Alice.

"What happened to you last night?"

"What do you mean?" she asked, terrified that Alice somehow knew about Frank and would think she was a whore.

"Where were you when I came back to get you?"

"You came back?"

"Didn't Bev tell you?"

"Tell me what?"

"Tina got sick and I had to run her home. I told Bev to tell you I would be back to get you."

"She must have been so wrapped up in Todd that she forgot."

Alice giggled, "He is a hunk. You didn't seem to mind the one you were with."

"I made a deal so I had to stick to it."

"A deal? What kind of a deal?"

"I had to promise to keep him company if Todd went over to Bev."

"I'd say that she owes you big time. How did you get home?"

"Frank drove me."

"How is our plan working?"

"Martin's still in the shower so I don't know yet."

"Call me and let me know."

She was hanging up the phone when Martin came into the kitchen. "Who was that?" he asked.

"Alice. Checking up on me to see if I'm still alive or if the hangover killed me."

"Tie one on last night?"

"Had a good time."

Nothing more was said as Martin dived into his eggs and bacon and she left the room to take a shower. As she used a soapy rag on her pussy she remembered how good it had felt when Frank had been in her and then she remembered he said he would call. And she remembered that she had not said, "No, please don't." She HAD said that she would like it if he did. Why had she done that? Why hadn't she fought him off? She had known it was wrong, but she had still allowed it. And then she had let him do it two more times and what was worse - she had loved it! When Frank had kissed her good night a block from the house, she realized that if he had suggested they get in the back seat again, she probably would have done it. How could she love Martin and do that? And she did love Martin; she was in no doubt about that.

But did Martin love her?

The memory of Frank in her pussy flooded in on her. No, no more of that! She was Martin's and by God, it was time to do something about that. She finished her shower, quickly dried off and then, still naked, she headed for the kitchen. She wasn't going to wait for Martin to notice her. No, damn it, she would force the issue. She would take him on the kitchen table if she had to. When she reached the kitchen, he was gone. She heard the garage door opened and she went to the window and saw him back out of the drive and head off to work. All right then, she would do it tonight. No matter what time he got home, she would be awake and waiting for him, naked and ready.

She dressed and called Alice and told her that she hadn't done the phone number thing. She lied and said that Martin had been in a rotten mood over something at work and she didn't think the time was right. They talked for a couple of more minutes and then she headed for the gym and her morning workout. She didn't see Todd there and she smiled to herself as she thought that Bev might not have left him enough strength to get out of bed that morning. Thinking about Todd brought Frank back to her mind, and she felt her pussy tingle again as she remembered her night in his car.

She had just taken a load of laundry out of the dryer when the phone rang. She answered it and it was Frank.

"I'm on my cell baby. I'm parked where we stopped last night and I can be there in sixty seconds."

No, she told herself, end this now and she took a deep breath and got ready to tell him "Thanks, but no thanks" but what came out was, "Hurry, I'll be waiting." She met him at the door naked and hurried him to the bedroom and helped him undress. She knew it was wrong and that she was giving away what should have been Martin's, but Martin didn't seem to want her and Frank did. She had worked so hard to make herself into something Martin would desire, but he ignored her. She had primed herself for sex and Martin did not seem to care at all about the new her. She was ready and she needed sex, Frank was there, Frank wanted her, and Frank was ready.

Their first coupling was frantic and frenzied and she clutched at him, pulled him to her, pushed up at him and begged him to fuck her. Words she had never used with Martin flowed from her like water from a faucet.

"Fuck me, push your cock deeper, fuck my cunt, fuck your slut, make me cum."

All the words she'd heard on the porn tapes became hers to use and she used them on Frank.

"Fuck me, fuck me, fuck me hard and make me cum" and Frank did his best to give her what she was demanding. She came twice before Frank moaned, "I can't hold back any longer" and then released in her. She hugged him to her as he drained and then he got off and said:

"Get me hard again baby."

She knew what he wanted and she had never done it before. She had planned on doing it to Martin the next time they made love, but the way things were going, only God knew when that would be or if it would ever happen at all. Well, she would practice on Frank and that way Martin would get her best when she did get him in bed. She thought about all the blow jobs she had seen on the porn tapes and then she tried to copy them.

When she took Frank's cock in her mouth, it was the first time she tasted cum. Actually, it wasn't cum, it was a mixture of her juices and Frank's sperm and the taste wasn't as bad as she'd imagined it would be. She licked Frank's cock clean and then licked all the juices from his balls. He moaned and she thought that the videos did a marvelous job of instruction. Once she had his cock licked clean she took it in her mouth, clamped her lips tight and started bobbing her head. Should she suck him all the way off and get an undiluted taste of sperm? A picture of Martin entered her mind and to herself she said no, she would save that for Martin.

Frank's soft cock began to harden and she gloried in being able to do that; to give the gift of life to Frank's cock. It was a great feeling. Why had she denied Martin and herself these pleasures all these years? Why had not Martin pushed her into doing these things? She knew the answer to those questions, even as she asked them - he loved her. He would never make her do anything that she didn't want to do and she had been a prude. God, how had Martin been able to stand her. She knew the answer to that one too. He stood it by ignoring her, but by God that was going to change. He wouldn't know what hit him!

She swung over Frank and like she had seen Angel Dust do on the videos she used one hand to guide Frank into her pussy as she settled down onto his hard cock. It was the first time she had ever been on top and she loved the sense of control it gave her. She slid up and down on Frank and rocked back and forth. More words she had never used before came out of her mouth:

"Oh God your cock feels so good in my pussy. I love the way your cock fills me."

Several pleasurable minutes went by and then Frank gripped her in his strong hands and rolled her onto her back and then he started fucking her as hard as he could. He was breathing hard and sweat dripped off him as he pounded into her pussy. She moaned and pushed herself up at him as an orgasm ripped through her body. He pushed hard and deep into her and her nails bit into Frank's back as her legs clamped tight around him.

Frank moaned and she felt the hot splash of his tribute to her. She held him tight as his cock softened and he gasped out:

"I don't think I'm ever going to get enough of you."

"Does that mean you want to go again?"

Oh Jesus yes. All I need is some time to recover enough to get it hard again."

"I'm afraid that I can't give you that much time. I want to go again too, but you need to go. I have to change the sheets and then shower before my husband gets home."

"When can I see you again?"

"Why Frank," she asked coyly, "Why would you ever want to see me again?"

"Because you are the hottest piece of ass I've ever had and I want more. I want much, much more."

"Well then, give me a number where I can reach you and I'll call when the opportunity arises."

She took the number from him, but she knew she would never call. What she had done with him was very enjoyable, but he was only a diversion. Martin was her target and if she did things right, she would never lack for a hard cock again as Martin would keep her very, very busy or she would keep him very busy, whatever!

<<O>>

Freshly showered and the bed was made, she dug through her closet looking for something sexy and enticing that she could wear when Martin came home from work. She found nothing. She suddenly realized that she wouldn't. She had never been one for sexy under garments or frilly things. She would have to do something about that. Maybe talk to Bev. Bev was always having lingerie parties, so she should be able to give her some idea of what was needed. She did have high heels though, so that would have to do. She would greet Martin at the door wearing nothing but high heels and hand him a chilled martini. That would certainly get his attention.

By six-thirty dinner was ready and so was she. Anticipation had her pussy wet and she wasn't sure that she would even let Martin eat his dinner. She might drag him straight to the bedroom or take him on the kitchen table, and she giggled at the thought of it.

At six thirty-five the phone rang and she answered it. When she hung up a tear was trickling down her cheek. God damn him and that fucking job of his! Another damned emergency out of town business trip. She made herself a drink, polished it off and made herself another. Halfway through it, she put it down and picked up the phone and punched in a number. When the call was answered, she said:

"Hello Frank. Busy tonight, or could you stop by."

Chapter Three

She was bent forward over her desk, skirt pushed up to her waist and her thong in a pile around her right ankle as I pushed my hard cock into her from behind. She had a file folder gripped between her teeth to keep her from crying out and letting everyone in the outer office know what was happening to her. I gripped her hips and drove hard into her, wanting to get as deep as I could before I came.

I still could not get over how readily this hot beauty would open herself to me and I took as much advantage of it as I could. One of these days I was going to have to make a choice and I was dreading it, but I just could not keep up with Beth, Angela and Cathy. Something had to give. The trouble was that I didn't want to give up any of them. Each one was gorgeous, each one was sexy, they all three fucked like nymphomaniacs and each one had their own little quirk.

Beth liked to do it where there was a chance of discovery; Angela loved taking it in the ass and Cathy was crazy about sucking cock. I d spent one night with her when that was all she did. I never fucked her once that night; all three loads went down her throat.

Between Beth, Angela, and Cathy I was surprised that I wasn't worn down to skin and bones. And it was lucky for me that I had a wife who was so disinterested in me that she never questioned my absences.

I sent my deposit into Beth's cunt and then held still until my cock started to soften and then I pulled myself out and bent to help Beth put her thong back on. She moved back behind her desk and then asked:

"What are you doing tonight?"

"Nothing that I know of."

"Can you take another out of town trip?"

"No problem. Jennie probably wouldn't even notice me if I was home anyway. Why?"

"My hubby is going out of town on business which is code for he is going to be in some other woman's bed. That means I need someone to keep me company in my bed tonight. I thought we might go out and celebrate and then go back to my place and celebrate some more."

"Celebrate what?"

"Your promotion to vice president."

"Me? A vice president? Why on Earth would you do that?"

"Because you have earned it. You brought Montrose back; you got Cartridge back and you landed Baxter. This company is alive because of you."

I thought about that for several seconds. Outside of cheating on Jennie, and that didn't count because she didn't care about me anyway, I had never been dishonest and there was no reason to start now.

"I would be a lousy vice president. A good regional manager maybe, but I'm nowhere near qualified to be a vice president."

"Nonsense Martin, look at what you have done?"

"That's just it Beth, I didn't do anything. Angela didn't want me; she wanted to see you crawl. Once you humbled yourself by having to ask me to help save the company you had her account back. She told me that I didn't even need to spend the weekend with her. All she wanted was to get back at you for stealing her boyfriend. She also told me that even if you hadn't crawled she would not have let you close the doors. I didn't do anything to get Cartridge back; Angela picked up the phone and called in a favor. Same with Baxter. She made a phone call and they called me. So far, all I have done is go along for the ride. No Beth, if you need a vice president go see Angela."

"Why are you telling me this? It isn't normal. Nobody turns down a huge promotion like that."

"Honey, I care for you and that means I have to care for your company. I would not, at least at this time, be good for the company as a vice president. Maybe some day, but not now. As for telling you about Angela, I'm doing it as a favor for both of you. Angela is hurting. She hides it well, but I've spent enough time with her and listened to her to know what I'm talking about. You grew up close as sisters and you only split apart because of the boyfriend. She misses you and what you had back then. She kept your company alive Beth, but she did it for you, not because of me."

She sat there and stared at me for several moments and then said, "Okay, then we will celebrate your promotion to regional manager."

I got up to leave and when I reached the door, she said, "Martin" and I turned back to her.

"Thank you Martin, thank you for everything."

I smiled at her and got back to work."

<<O>>

At lunch time, I picked up the phone and called home. Jennie answered and I told her the lie that I had told her so often. I told her I would be flying to Dallas that afternoon and wouldn't be back until the next day. There was silence on the other end of the line for a moment or two and I asked:

"Jennie? Are you still there?"

"Yes Martin, I'm here. Martin, you need to come home. I need you."

"You need me Jennie? Why now? You have spent the last couple of years ignoring me; why do you need me now?"

"Just come home Martin. Quit your stupid job if you have to, but come home."

"I'm not quitting my job Jennie. I'll see you tomorrow and we can talk about it then."

I lowered the handset and shook my head. She needed me? She had never said that to me before. As I put the handset in the cradle I wondered what the hell was going on. Oh well, I'd find out the next day.

<<O>>

She hung up the phone and then stared at the wall for several seconds before going back to cleaning the house. It looked like the only way she was going to get Martin's attention was go down to his office and lay down naked on his desk. Face up to it girl, she said to herself, he doesn't want you. All that hard work to get him back to where you could... shit! Goddamn him. Just then, the phone rang. It was Frank asking her if she would like some company. She had promised herself the last time she had been with him that that was the end of it, but what the hell, he at least wanted her.

"Sure Frank, hurry on over."

She hung up the phone and headed for the bedroom to turn down the covers and get naked. She met him at the door naked and as soon as the door closed behind him she was on her knees in front of him and taking his cock out. She took him in her mouth and sucked on him and when he was fully erect, she stood up, took his cock in her hand and led him into the bedroom.

Frank fucked her through two orgasms before he came and as she was working on getting him up again he said:

"How come you have never asked me to eat your pussy?"

"I've been told that a lot of men don't like to do that. How come you've never asked?"

"Because I've always been too eager to bury my cock in that hot pussy of yours that I've never got around to asking and you never indicated any interest."

She took her mouth off his cock and rolled over on her back and spread her legs. "Help yourself," she said.

As Frank lowered his face to her pussy, she had the thought that she was about to have another new experience that she had planned for Martin to do. Sex cowgirl style, reverse cowgirl, doggie, missionary but with legs up on the man's shoulders, sucking cock and now having her pussy eaten - all things that Martin was supposed to do, but was never around to do.

She shivered as Frank's tongue licked along her pussy lips and then she moaned as his tongue parted those lips and began to probe. Oh God, why had she stopped Martin when he tried to do this to her. She spread her legs wide as he licked and sucked on her pussy. Her heels were planted firmly on the bed and she pushed herself up at Frank's mouth.

Frank worked one finger into her pussy and then two. He found her clit and sucked on it as he fingered her and she felt the fire building deep inside her and then suddenly her body shook when the orgasm hit her. She cried out and Frank abandoned his efforts on her cunt and he moved up and drove his cock into her. "Oh yessss," she moaned as he pushed his cock in deep. Her legs came up and clamped his waist and her hands grabbed at the cheeks of his ass and she tried to pull him even deeper into her. She was grunting, "Yes, yes, yes, yes" as Frank slammed his cock into her.

Another orgasm started forming in her core and she cried out, "Fuck me hard Frank, fuck me, fuck me hard." Frank rammed himself into her and her orgasm rushed in on her and she clutched at Frank as her body shook and seconds later she felt him splash her insides. She continued to hold him tightly until his cock started to soften and then she let her legs and arms fall to the bed. Frank rolled off her and kissed her neck.

"You are one hot momma and I'm so glad I found you."

His fingers stroked the lips of her pussy and she moaned. "Want more huh" Frank asked as he turned his body and pushed his face into her crotch. She saw his cock swaying above her face and she knew that Frank wanted to sixty-nine with her. She felt his mouth on her sex and she opened her legs. As he started licking her wet, cum filled pussy, his hips lowered his cock towards her face and she opened her mouth and accepted him.

She was amazed at how quickly her sucking and licking had hardened Frank's cock and as soon as he was stiff he turned around to get into position to fuck her again. She spread her legs wide, but he told her to get up on her hands and knees and then his cock speared into her from behind. She had two more orgasms before Frank came again.

She was laying there looking up at the ceiling while catching her breath when it occurred to her that Martin had never given her an orgasm. But then she had never really given him a chance to give her one. This was wrong, so wrong. Everything that Martin was supposed to be getting was being enjoyed by Frank. It wasn't right, but then again, Martin didn't want her.

"Another thing we have never done" he said as he moved between her legs for the third time that afternoon, "Is anal. Want to do it now?"

She wanted to, oh yes indeed she wanted to and she was on the verge of telling him yes, but to go slow and take it easy, but what came out was:

"No Frank, my ass belongs to my husband."

Why did she say that? Even as she asked, she knew the answer. She had to save something for Martin that would only ever be his. Frank shrugged and pushed his cock into her and she moaned as he started to fuck her.

<<O>>

As usual, Maxine's was crowded. It was a good thing that Beth had made reservations. They were in a booth and were sipping a good Chardonnay. They had just given their order and when the waiter was gone, Beth asked:

"Just how much do you know about the situation between Angela and me?"

"Only what she told me. The two of you were tight until you married her boyfriend. She did say she was glad you did it, since he turned out to be a cheating asshole. She also said she didn't think you had a clue that he was running around on you."

"Oh, I have more than a clue. I got suspicious of him before the first year of our marriage was out. I hired private detectives to follow him and they got me all the dirt on him."

"Why didn't you get rid of him?"

"It would cause me more trouble than its worth. It would have tied up assets at a time when I couldn't afford to have those assets tied up. I settled for going on the pill and using a diaphragm to make sure there were no kids, and then I got on with running the company. I'll get rid of him if I meet someone I think I can go the distance with.

"I called Angela this afternoon Martin. Thank you for making that possible. If you haven't said what you did this morning, it never would have happened. I missed her, I really have. Well sweetie, you have solved most of my problems, what can we do about yours?"

"I don't know if anything can be done about mine. I love Jennie, but she has no interest in me and as a result, I have distanced myself from her to reduce the hurt. I can't leave her, but I can barely stand to be around her."

Our order came and the conversation waned as we ate. I had just topped off Beth's wine glass when she put down her fork and said:

"Oh shit!"

"What?"

"That couple being seated over there" she pointed as she said, "That's my husband."

I turned and looked and I'm sure my face paled. "Double oh shit," I said, "That's my wife."

"That's your wife? The one who has let herself go? The one who has allowed herself to become so unattractive? Are you on drugs Martin? She is a fox and if she is with my husband, she can't be as cold in bed as you, because Frank doesn't hang with women like that. And from the way they are holding hands, I'd say that they didn't just meet today."

It didn't look that way to me either. "Maybe that's why she hasn't been interested in me; she has someone else all along."

"Well she hasn't had him long. I check up on Frank from time to time to keep the file current for when I dump him and your wife isn't the one he was sleeping with, at least not up till the end of last month. I knew he had a new honey, but he usually keeps them for about six months so I haven't been in a hurry to put the private detectives on him. She's fairly recent. What are you going to do?"

"What are you going to do?"

"Nothing. Just hope he doesn't notice me and decide to create a scene. I don't think he will do that though, he likes my money too much. My bet is that, if he does notice us, he will pretend he didn't and hope that I didn't notice him. But I am more than ready to throw him out if you want to confront them."

"How can I do that? I'm supposed to be out of town."

"You lie. The trip was cancelled at the last minute; I asked you to have a working dinner with me to go over some scheduling issues, you called home and got no answer and you came in here and there she was. You just need to make up your mind. But as you do it, be aware of one thing, if she is with Frank then he is fucking her. Frank does not waste time on girls who don't put out."

"I don't do public scenes. When we are done and are ready to go, you can leave and then I'll swing by their table and let her know she has been caught. That way, you won't be involved."

"Oh no sweetie, if you are going to do that, them I'm going to do it with you. I got a new start with Angela today and I might as well make the day a total success and get started on a new life - a life without Frank. After you stop by their table, what are you going to do?"

"I guess that will pretty much depend on her."

"I mean for tonight?"

"We already have a plan for that, don't we? I'm sure not in any mood to go home and you did invite me to spend the night."

"Yes I did, but are you going to be any fun?"

"I'll do my best, but then again - maybe spending the night at your place might not be a good idea."

"Why not?"

"Won't Frank rush home and try to salvage something?"

"Not Mr. Macho. He won't allow himself to be seen coming hat in hand. He will wait a couple of days and then call me to talk and try to convince me that it is all a misunderstanding. By then, I'll have the locks changed at the house and a restraining order against him."

"Okay, your place it is."

We finished our meal in silence and I wondered what I had done that my wife wouldn't have sex with me, but instead with another man. I wasn't blind. I'd seen the changes in her, but she still stayed distant. I wondered who she had been seeing before Frank. Who had caused her to make changes in herself? Well, I would probably get the answers to those questions in the next couple of days and I was pretty sure I wasn't going to like what I heard.

Beth and I passed on dessert and I called for the check. Once the credit card slip was signed, I asked Beth:

"Are you sure you want this? You could still get out before I go over there."

"No sweetie, it is time to end the farce. I'm ready if you are."

"Okay, let's do it."

Frank had been smiling at her when all of a sudden the smile disappeared.

"Good evening Jennie" she heard and turned to see Martin standing there with a woman.

"Martin! What are you doing here?"

"How interesting, I was just about to ask you the same question. My trip got cancelled at the last minute and my boss asked me to have a working dinner with her to discuss some scheduling issues. I tried calling the house to let you know I would be home, but I got no answer. I now see why. Is this what you do on all my out of town trips? Oh, excuse my manners. Jennie, this is my boss Beth. Beth, this is my about to be ex-wife Jennie."

"I would say pleased to meet you Jennie, if it wasn't my about to be ex-husband you are sitting with. I must say that you do make an attractive couple sitting there holding hands. Would you walk me to my car Martin? I would like to put some distance between me and Frank."

"I must say that I have the same feeling. No need to cut short your evening and rush home Jennie; I won't be there."

As Martin and Frank's wife turned to walk away she said, "Martin, please Martin, I can ex…" but he kept on walking and didn't acknowledge that he heard her.

"Oh my God," she cried, "How did I let this happen? What am I going to do?"

"Obviously, since he said he wasn't going to be home, we can safely spend the night together."

"Are you out of your mind?!!"

"No, just being realistic. We're busted so there isn't any sense crying about it."

"You never told me you were married; you aren't wearing a ring."

"So I'm married, so what? So are you, or had you forgotten."

"Oh my God, I might lose my husband and you sit over there acting like it means nothing."

She picked up her purse and got up from the table. "Where are you going" Frank asked.

"Home so I can be there when he does show up."

"Wait up, I'll go with you."

"Oh no you won't. I don't want anything to do with you anymore."

She hurried outside, flagged down a cab and gave her address to the driver. Then she sat back in the seat and the tears began to flow.

<<O>>

"What now" Beth asked.

"Get through the night, work a full day tomorrow and then go home."

"Go home and do what?"

"I don't honestly know. Being an outraged husband is not an option. I'm not a hypocrite and I can't very well rage at her considering what I've been doing. I will try and find out why she cut me off, started ignoring me and then took up with your husband. For all I know he isn't the first. I may try and find out who and how many."

"Is there a divorce in your future?"

"It is possible, very possible."

"I think you will be happier in one of the guest bedrooms tonight sweetie. I'd love to have you in my bed tonight, but I don't really think that all of you would be there."

"You are probably right."

I slept fitfully, which is to say I got almost no sleep at all. I could not for the life of me understand what had happened to Jennie. What had I done for her to do to me what she did?

Three cups of coffee didn't do much to start the day off and as I waited for Beth I saw that she hadn't wasted any time in getting started on Frank. It was only seven in the morning and a van with Acoma Locks painted on the side was pulling into the circular drive up front.

On the way to work Beth asked me if I had given any more thought to whether I was going for a divorce or not.

"That's the second time you have asked me that. Why?"

"Because your alimony will be based on what you make. I can hold off on that raise I am going to give you until after the divorce is final and that way you won't get hosed so bad."

"Thanks for the thought, but a raise to regional manager's pay isn't going to be all that significant."

"Maybe not a regional manager's pay, but that's not what I intend to give you. You won't take a promotion to vice president, but you are going to get a vice president's salary and benefits. You saved my company sweetie. You can "Aw shucks, it wasn't really me" all you want, but it wouldn't have happened without you and you know it. It all happened because you - you Martin - you said you would help me with my Angela problem. Everything that happened resulted in your agreement to help me, and you will never convince me otherwise, so don't even try."

"Yes, ma'am."

"There, that wasn't so hard, was it?"

It was a long day at work and I wasn't sure I even earned my pay as my mind was elsewhere. It was on my life and where it was going. On Jennie and what had happened between us. On what I had done to make the change in her. How had she gone from a missionary only prude, into having an affair or affairs? Who had been the one who caused her to do something about her appearance? Who? Why? I wanted to know. I needed to know. Jennie had called twice that day and I told her that I wouldn't talk to her until I came home that night to pack. She had cried, "Pack?!! Oh God no Martin, ple..." and I hung up on her.

The answers to the questions were at the house, but by the end of the day, I had to force myself to go home to get them.

She had screwed up and she knew it. She had no one else but herself to blame and she knew that also, but she loved Martin and she didn't not want to live without him in her life. How could she save anything out of the mess she had made? Her only hope was that he would listen to her as she tried to explain what had led her to do what she had done, believe her when she told him how much she loved him and that he would give her the forgiveness she would beg for.

The one thing she did know was that she had to be completely honest with him. She would not sugar coat the pill on what she had done with Frank. She would not tell Martin that she was just having dinner with a friend. No, Martin would get it all, no matter how bad it made her look. She owed the man she loved that much, at least.

She knew that the mood of Martin once he came home, will not be good, so she didn't bother to make dinner. There would be no sitting down, eating in silence and then going:

"Okay, what would you like to talk about?"

If she wanted to keep Martin, she has to do something to blunt the anger he would be bringing home with him. She would have to distract him long enough to give her time to get it all out before he went on the attack. She thought long and hard on it and finally decided the best thing to do would be to do the last thing he would expect.

She was sitting where she could see him, when he pulled into the drive. She was as ready as she could be. She took a deep breath and prayed that it would work, and that she could get Martin back before she lost him.

I still had no idea of how I was going to handle it when I opened the door and walked into the house. I stopped in my tracks at the sight that greeted me. Jennie stood there in a sheer black teddy and 'Come Fuck Me' pumps with four inch heels and holding a filled martini glass out to me. Dumbfounded, I reached out and took it from her hand.

"Would you like your blowjob before my explanation or after?"

My mind wasn't working. This wasn't my Jennie. I stood there holding the martini as she said:

"I'll take that as you want it first" and she knelt down in front of me, pulled down my zipper and had a hand on my cock before I got myself together enough to say:

"Damn it Jennie, this is no…" and that was as far as I got before her hot mouth enveloped me. "Oh shit" I thought as I felt her tongue work on me, "It is the only blow job I will ever get from her so I might as well enjoy it." I looked down to see her looking up at me as her head moved back and forth on my cock. I saw her hands undoing my belt and my trousers fell to the floor. She took her mouth off of me, long enough to pull my briefs down and then her mouth captured me again.

With my briefs out of the way, her left hand fondled my nuts and I moaned as she took my cock all the way to the back of her throat. Her right hand went to my ass and she teased my butt hole with a finger and I groaned as the cum rushed out of me and into her mouth. She didn't pull back. Both of her hands gripped my ass and she held me as she swallowed my discharge and then she held me in her mouth until I became limp. She stood up, took the martini from my hand and took a sip and then handed the glass back to me.

"I want very much to kiss you right now Martin, but given what I just did, I don't want to gross you out. You might not like the taste of yourself."

"What the hell is this all about Jennie?"

"I wanted to relax you Martin. I wanted to relax you enough that you will sit down and give me a chance to save my marriage. I heard you introduce me to your boss last night as your "about to be ex-wife" and I want to change your mind if I can."

"Why the hell do you want to save our marriage Jennie? You have spent the last couple of years not showing any interest in me whatever. Why, after I find out about you having other men in your life, are you suddenly so interested in keeping me?"

She knelt down in front of me again and said, "Step out of your pants Martin" and then she pulled them out of the way as I lifted my feet. As she stood up, she stuck her tongue out and licked my cock and it twitched. It wanted her mouth again.

"Take a sip of your martini Martin and come sit down and I'll tell you everything."

I followed her into the family room and sat down on the couch. She took the easy chair across from me and said:

"I want to save our marriage Martin because I love you. I have never loved anyone but you and I want to stay with you."

"What about Frank?"

"Frank was a mistake Martin, a stupid mistake made by a stupid woman who was upset because her husband ignored her and wouldn't have anything to do with her. A woman who thought her husband didn't want her any more. I was vulnerable; Frank saw it and he took advantage of the situation. I could have said no, but I didn't."

"Why would you think I didn't want you anymore?"

"When was the last time you made love to me Martin?"

"I don't remember."

"Exactly my point Martin. Oh, I know why you lost interest in me. I know that I didn't look all that appealing and even when we made love I was a prude. Making love felt nice, but it wasn't all that big a thing to me. It was something that I could take or leave. And as I let myself go, you didn't push for sex and since I was so-so on the subject anyway, I said nothing and things slid away from us.

"It wasn't until I joined that book discussion group at the library and was befriended by Alice and the others that things changed for me."

I sat there and listened as she told the story of the video tapes and how they made her want to try things with me, of looking in the mirror and suddenly realizing why I didn't bother her for sex anymore and how she set out to bring me back to her.

"I worked hard Martin, I busted my ass to make myself appealing to you, but you never noticed. You never commented on the change in me, not once. All you had time for was your job. Other men were looking at me, other men were making passes at me, but I couldn't even get you to acknowledge that there was a change in me. I got bitter Martin. I did all that work to make myself better for you, but you couldn't be bothered. I made up my mind that I had worked hard enough to get myself in shape for you, but I'd be damned if I was going to crawl to you and demand that you look at me. By God, you were going to have to come to me. I know now that that was stupid of me. If I had forced the issue we wouldn't be where we are now."

She told me how Alice had noticed her being out of sorts and how she had told Alice everything and how Alice had come up with the phone numbers plan. She told me of the night at the bar and how she had gloried in the attention she got.

"They wanted me Martin; every one of them wanted me, but you didn't. I was primed and ready Martin. The tapes had set me on the path to wanting to give you the love life you deserved, but you didn't seem to want me. You just didn't seem to care about me at all. I'm not blaming all the drinks I had that night, although they probably had something to do with lowering my inhibitions, but I was primed and ready to be fucked Martin and I let my good sense get away from me and Frank was there to pounce.

"I knew it was stupid and when I got home, I was sorry as hell that I'd done it. The next morning I made up my mind to force the issue and while you were eating breakfast, I took a quick shower and then hurried naked back to the kitchen, but you had already gone. Last night I was going to meet you at the door the way I did tonight, but then you called and said you were going out of town again. I asked you to come home and I told you that I needed you and you pushed me away again. Five minutes after you hung up Frank called and I thought, "At least someone wants me" and I agreed to have dinner with him knowing that we would probably end up in a motel. We went to the restaurant and the rest you know."

"Why would you go to a motel since you knew I wouldn't be coming home?"

"Your house and your bed Martin. I couldn't do it here, I just couldn't."

"So you are saying that this is all my fault? That I caused you to do fuck another man?"

"No, that isn't what I'm saying. I accept that I'm responsible for what I did. What I'm doing is explaining how it happened and I'm hoping you will understand why it happened. I made a monumentally stupid mistake and I'm begging you to forgive me. Please Martin I love you, God knows I do and I hope you do too. Just give me a chance to prove it Martin. That is all I'm asking for, your forgiveness and a chance."

I stared at her and thought about our situation. I had thought she was disinterested when what she was doing was waiting for me to say, "Wow, what have you done to yourself." I had noticed the changes and thought they were for someone else. Talk about two people lacking in communication skills. And what about what I had been doing. A pot calling the kettle black situation if there ever was one.

I loved her; I had always loved her, even when she had seemed disinterested. Should I tell her what I had been doing? Show her that we were even? No, I didn't think so. It might not make things better and in fact, it could make things worse. I wanted to give her what she wanted, the forgiveness she was asking for, but first I had to know.

"Was Frank the only one or were there others?"

"There was no one else Martin, no one!"

"And Frank got all the benefit of your newfound sexuality?"

She blushed and then she said, "No, not all of it. He got my first blow job and it was a pretty poor one since it was my first, but I learned from it though and the one you just got was a lot better. And he did get me into some positions other than missionary. He wanted all of it, but I did save one thing just for you."

"What?"

"He wanted my ass Martin, but I told him the only one who would ever go there would be you."

<<O>>

She looked at him, unable to read what he was thinking by looking at his face. She had deliberately lied in indicating that she and Frank had only done it the one time. She felt hat was confession enough. It wouldn't help matters any for Martin to know of than other times and he didn't need to know how far she had gone on those times and he sure did not need to know that any of it was in his house and on his bed.

Let him believe he would be the first on most of it. If he stayed she would make it up to him. She promised herself if he stayed he would never regret it, not for one second. She had painted herself as a cheat and she knew she had shocked him by being as forward as she had been, but she didn't know if it had worked. "Please God," she prayed, "Let him forgive me."

<<O>>

"Hey girlfriend, how are you doing" Alice asked.

"Not bad," Jennie said, "I'm hanging in there."

"The reason I'm calling is to let you know that Tina won't be playing cards with us tonight. She's coming down with something. She thinks it's the flu. I've lined up a sub for her though. We still on for seven?"

"Yes."

"What's the matter? You sound a little down."

"Every once in a while it catches up with me. The things that happened and the way things went."

"Buck up girlfriend, you'll survive. See you tonight."

She put down the phone and got busy cleaning the place up and preparing the refreshments. The doorbell rang at six forty-five and she answered it to find Alice and another woman standing there. The woman looked familiar and it took her a second or two to recognize her.

"Oh my God, it's you, it really is you."

"Surprise, surprise," Alice said. "Norma, meet Jennie. Jennie, meet Norma, also known to us as Angel Dust. She is in town to visit family and I asked her to fill in for Tina."

"Well, come on in. Don't just stand there, come in, come in. Honey, come here a minute."

"What" asked Martin as he walked into the room.

"Honey, I would like you to meet Norma. Norma, this is my husband Martin and next to me he is one of your biggest fans."

"I am?"

"You sure are. You watch her at least once a week."

"I do?"

Alice laughed and said, "Try and imagine her without her clothes on."

He stared at Norma and suddenly the light bulb went on over his head and he stepped forward and extended his hand as said:

"Welcome to our humble abode."

Jennie took Norma's hand and said, "Follow me into the kitchen and while I'm making you a drink, I'll tell you how you almost ruined my marriage and then saved it."

As Jennie led Norma away Alice asked, "What was that all about? What did I miss?"

"Long story, but you will have to get it from Jennie."

"You two seem to be getting along fine."

"We are. By the way, I never have thanked you for trying to help. Even though Jennie never did get to use the phone number ploy you did try to help and I appreciate it."

"Hey, what are friends for? So, how does it feel knowing that you are going to be a daddy?"

"It still hasn't caught up to me yet. Come on. Let's get the other two and play some Euchre."

She was bent forward over her desk, skirt pushed up to her waist and her thong in a pile around her right ankle as I pushed my hard cock into her from behind. She had a file folder gripped between her teeth to keep her from crying out and letting everyone in the outer office know what was happening to her. I gripped her hips and drove hard into her wanting to get as deep as I could before I came.

I still could not get over how readily this hot beauty would open herself for me and I took as much advantage of it as I could. One of these days I was going to have to make a choice and I was dreading it, but I just could not keep up with Beth, Angela and Cathy. Something had to give. The trouble was that I didn't want to give up any of them. Each one was gorgeous, each one was sexy, they all three fucked like nymphomaniacs and each one had their own little quirk.

Beth liked to do it where there was a chance of discovery; Angela loved taking it in the ass and Cathy was crazy about sucking cock. I d spent one night with her when that was all she did. I never fucked her once that night; all three loads went down her throat.

Between Beth, Angela, and Cathy I was surprised that I wasn't worn down to skin and bones. And it was lucky for me that I had a wife who was so disinterested in me that she never questioned my absences.

I sent my deposit into Beth's cunt and then held still until my cock started to soften and then I pulled myself out and bent to help Beth put her thong back on. She moved back behind her desk and then asked:

"What are you doing tonight?"

"Nothing that I know of."

"Can you take another out of town trip?"

"No problem. Jennie probably wouldn't even notice me if I was home anyway. Why?"

"My hubby is going out of town on business which is code for he is going to be in some other woman's bed. That means I need someone to keep me company in my bed tonight. I thought we might go out and celebrate and then go back to my place and celebrate some more."

"Celebrate what?"

"Your promotion to vice president."

"Me? A vice president? Why on Earth would you do that?"

"Because you have earned it. You brought Montrose back; you got Cartridge back and you landed Baxter. This company is alive because of you."

I thought about that for several seconds. Outside of cheating on Jennie, and that didn't count because she didn't care about me anyway, I had never been dishonest and there was no reason to start now.

"I would be a lousy vice president. A good regional manager maybe, but I'm nowhere near qualified to be a vice president."

"Nonsense Martin, look at what you have done?"

"That's just it Beth, I didn't do anything. Angela didn't want me; she wanted to see you crawl. Once you humbled yourself by having to ask me to help save the company you had her account back. She told me that I didn't even need to spend the weekend with her. All she wanted was to get back at you for stealing her boyfriend. She also told me that even if you hadn't crawled she would not have let you close the doors. I didn't do anything to get Cartridge back; Angela picked up the phone and called in a favor. Same with Baxter. She made a phone call and they called me. So far all I have done is go along for the ride. No Beth, if you need a vice president go see Angela."

"Why are you telling me this? It isn't normal. Nobody turns down a huge promotion like that."

"Honey, I care for you and that means I have to care for your company. I would not, at least at this time, be good for the company as a vice president. Maybe someday but not now. As for telling you about Angela, I'm doing it as a favor for both of you. Angela is hurting. She hides it well, but I've spent enough time with her and listened to her to know what I'm talking about. You grew up close as sisters and you only split apart because of the boyfriend. She misses you and what you had back then. She kept your company alive Beth, but she did it for you, not because of me."

She sat there and stared at me for several moments and then said, "Okay, then we will celebrate your promotion to regional manager."

I got up to leave and when I reached the door, she said, "Martin" and I turned back to her.

"Thank you Martin, thank you for everything."

I smiled at her and got back to work."

At lunch time I picked up the phone and called home. Jennie answered and I told her the lie that I had told her so often. I told her I would be flying to Dallas that afternoon and wouldn't be back until the next day. There was silence on the other end of the line for a moment or two and I asked:

"Jennie? Are you still there?"

"Yes Martin, I'm here. Martin, you need to come home. I need you."

"You need me Jennie? Why now? You have spent the last couple of years ignoring me; why do you need me now?"

"Just come home Martin. Quit your stupid job if you have to, but come home."

"I'm not quitting my job Jennie. I'll see you tomorrow and we can talk about it then."

I lowered the handset and shook my head. She needed me? She had never said that to me before. As I put the handset in the cradle I wondered what the hell was going on. Oh well, I'd find out the next day.

<<O>>

She hung up the phone and then stared at the wall for several seconds before going back to cleaning house. It looked like the only way she was going to get Martin's attention was go down to his office and lay down naked on his desk. Face up to it girl, she said to herself, he doesn't want you. All that hard work to get him back to where you could... shit! Goddamn him. Just then the phone rang. It was Frank asking her if she would like some company. She had promised herself the last time she had been with him that that was the end of it, but what the hell, he at least wanted her.

"Sure Frank, hurry on over."

She hung up the phone and headed for the bedroom to turn down the covers and get naked. She met him at the door naked and as soon as the door closed behind him she was on her knees in front of him and taking his cock out. She took him in her mouth and sucked on him and when he was fully erect she stood up, took his cock in her hand and led him into the bedroom.

Frank fucked her through two orgasms before he came and as she was working on getting him up again he said:

"How come you have never asked me to eat your pussy?"

"I've been told that a lot of men don't like to do that. How come you've never asked?"

"Because I've always been too eager to bury my cock in that hot pussy of yours that I've never got around to asking and you never indicated any interest."

She took her mouth off his cock and rolled over on her back and spread her legs. "Help yourself," she said.

As Frank lowered his face to her pussy she had the thought that she was about to have another new experience that she had planned on Martin doing. Sex cowgirl style, reverse cowgirl, doggie, missionary but with legs up on the man's shoulders, sucking cock and now having her pussy eaten - all things that Martin was supposed to do, but was never around to do.

She shivered as Frank's tongue licked along her pussy lips and then she moaned as his tongue parted those lips and began to probe. Oh God, why had she stopped Martin when he tried to do this to her. She spread her legs wide as he licked and sucked on her pussy. Her heels were planted firmly on the bed and she pushed herself up at Frank's mouth.

Frank worked one finger into her pussy and then two. He found her clit and sucked on it as he fingered her and she felt the fire building deep inside her and then suddenly her body shook when the orgasm hit her. She cried out and Frank abandoned his efforts on her cunt and he moved up and drove his cock into her. "Oh yessss," she moaned as he pushed his cock in deep. Her legs came up and clamped his waist and her hands grabbed at the cheeks of his ass and she tried to pull him even deeper into her. She was grunting, "Yes, yes, yes, yes" as Frank slammed his cock into her.

Another orgasm started forming in her core and she cried out, "Fuck me hard Frank, fuck me, fuck me hard." Frank rammed himself into her and her orgasm rushed in on her and she clutched at Frank as her body shook and seconds later she felt him splash her insides. She continued to hold him tightly until his cock started to soften and then she let her legs and arms fall to the bed. Frank rolled off her and kissed her neck.

"You are one hot momma and I'm so glad I found you."

His fingers stroked the lips of her pussy and she moaned. "Want more huh" Frank asked as he turned his body and pushed his face into her crotch. She saw his cock swaying above her face and she knew that Frank wanted to sixty-nine with her. She felt his mouth on her sex and she opened her legs. As he started licking her wet, cum filled pussy his hips lowered his cock towards her face and she opened her mouth and accepted him.

She was amazed at how quickly her sucking and licking had hardened Frank's cock and as soon as he was stiff he turned around to get into position to fuck her again. She spread her legs wide, but he told her to get up on her hands and knees and then his cock speared into her from behind. She had two more orgasms before Frank came again.

She was laying there looking up at the ceiling while catching her breath when it occurred to her that Martin had never given her an orgasm. But then she had never really given him a chance to give her one. This was wrong, so wrong. Everything that Martin was supposed to be getting was being enjoyed by Frank. It wasn't right, but then again, Martin didn't want her.

"Another thing we have never done" he said as he moved between her legs for the third time that afternoon, "Is anal. Want to do it now?"

She wanted to, oh yes indeed she wanted to and she was on the verge of telling him yes, but to go slow and take it easy, but what came out was:

"No Frank, my ass belongs to my husband."

Why did she say that? Even as she asked, she knew the answer. She had to save something for Martin that would only ever be his. Frank shrugged and pushed his cock into her and she moaned as he started to fuck her.

<<O>>

Maxine's was crowded as usual and it was a good thing that Beth had made reservations. They were in a booth and were sipping a good Chardonnay. They had just given their orders and when the waiter was gone, Beth asked:

"Just how much do you know about the situation between Angela and me?"

"Only what she told me. The two of you were tight until you married her boyfriend. She did say she was glad you did it since he turned out to be a cheating asshole. She also said she didn't think you had a clue that he was running around on you."

"Oh I have more than a clue. I got suspicious of him before the first year of our marriage was out. I put private detectives on him and they got me all the dirt on him."

"Why didn't you get rid of him?"

"It would have been more trouble than it would have been worth. It would have tied up assets at a time when I couldn't afford to have those assets tied up. I settled for going on the pill AND using a diaphragm to make sure there were no kids and then I got on with running the company. I'll get rid of him if I ever meet someone I think I can go the distance with.

"I called Angela this afternoon Martin. Thank you for making that possible. If you hadn't said what you did this morning it never would have happened. I've missed her, I really have. Well sweetie, you have solved most of my problems, what can we do about yours?"

"I don't know if anything can be done about mine. I love Jennie, but she has no interest in me and as a result I have distanced myself from her to reduce the hurt. I can't leave her, but I can barely stand to be around her."

Our order came and the conversation waned as we ate. I had just topped off Beth's wine glass when she put down her fork and said:

"Oh shit!"

"What?"

"That couple being seated over there" and she pointed as she said, "That's my husband."

I turned and looked and I'm sure my face paled. "Double oh shit," I said, "That's my wife."

"That's your wife? The one who has let herself go? The one who has allowed herself to become so unattractive? Are you on drugs Martin? She is a fox and if she is with my husband she can't be as cold in bed as you because Frank doesn't hang with women like that. And from the way they are holding hands I'd say that they didn't just meet today."

It didn't look that way to me either. "Maybe that's why she hasn't been interested in me; she has had someone else all along."

"Well she hasn't had him long. I check up on Frank from time to time to keep the file current for when I dump him and your wife isn't the one he was sleeping with, at least not up till the end of last month. I knew he had a new honey, but he usually keeps them for about six months so I haven't been in a hurry to put the private detectives on him. She's fairly recent. What are you going to do?"

"What are you going to do?"

"Nothing. Just hope he doesn't notice me and decide to create a scene. I don't think he will do that though, he likes my money too much. My bet is that if he does notice us he will pretend he didn't and hope that I didn't notice him. But I am more than ready to throw him out if you want to confront them."

"How can I do that? I'm supposed to be out of town."

"You lie. The trip was cancelled at the last minute; I asked you to have a working dinner with me to go over some scheduling issues, you called home and got no answer and you came in here and there she was. You just need to make up your mind, but as you do it be aware of one thing - if she is with Frank he is fucking her. Frank does not waste time on girls who don't put out."

"I don't do public scenes. When we are done and are ready to go you can leave and then I'll swing by their table and let her know she has been caught. That way you won't be involved."

"Oh no sweetie, if you are going to do that them I'm going to do it with you. I got a new start with Angela today and I might as well make the day a total success and get started on a new life - a life without Frank. After you stop by their table what are you going to do?"

"I guess that will pretty much depend on her."

"I mean for tonight?"

"We already have a plan for that, don't we? I'm sure not in any mood to go home and you did invite me to spend the night."

"Yes I did, but are you going to be any fun?"

"I'll do my best, but then again - maybe spending the night at your place might not be a good idea."

"Why not?"

"Won't Frank rush home and try to salvage something?"

"Not Mr. Macho. He won't allow himself to be seen coming hat in hand. He will wait a couple of days and then call asking to talk and try to convince me that it is all a misunderstanding. By then I'll have the locks changed at the house and a restraining order against him."

"Okay, your place it is."

We finished our meal in silence and I wondered what I had done that my wife wouldn't have sex with me, but would with another man. I wasn't blind. I'd seen the changes in her, but she still stayed distant. I wondered who she had been seeing before Frank. Who had caused her to make changes in herself? Well. I would probably get the answers to those questions in the next couple of days and I was pretty sure I wasn't going to like what I heard.

Beth and I passed on dessert and I called for the check. Once the credit card slip was signed I asked Beth:

"Are you sure you want this? You could still get out before I go over there."

"No sweetie, it is time to end the farce. I'm ready if you are."

"Okay, let's do it."

<<O>>

Frank had been smiling at her when all of a sudden the smile disappeared.

"Good evening Jennie" she heard and she turned to see Martin standing there with a woman.

"Martin! What are you doing here?"

"How interesting, I was just about to ask you the same question. My trip got cancelled at the last minute and my boss asked me to have a working dinner with her to discuss some scheduling issues. I tried calling the house to let you know I would be home, but I got no answer. I now see why. Is this what you do with all my out of town trips? Oh, excuse my manners. Jennie, this is my boss Beth. Beth, this is my about to be ex-wife Jennie."

"I would say pleased to meet you Jennie, if it wasn't my about to be ex-husband you are sitting with. I must say that you do make an attractive couple sitting there holding hands. Would you walk me to my car Martin? I would like to put some distance between me and Frank."

"I must say that I have the same feeling. No need to cut short your evening and rush home Jennie; I won't be there."

As Martin and Frank's wife turned to walk away she said, "Martin, please Martin, I can ex…" but he kept on walking and didn't acknowledge that he heard her.

"Oh my God," she cried, "How did I let this happen? What am I going to do?"

"Obviously, since he said he wasn't going to be home, we can safely spend the night together."

"Are you out of your mind?!!"

"No, just being realistic. We're busted so there isn't any sense crying about it."

"You never told me you were married; you aren't wearing a ring."

"So I'm married, so what? So are you, or had you forgotten."

"Oh my God, I might lose my husband and you sit over there acting like it means nothing."

She picked up her purse and got up from the table. "Where are you going" Frank asked.

"Home so I can be there when he does show up."

"Wait up, I'll go with you."

"Oh no you won't. I don't want anything to do with you anymore."

She hurried outside, flagged down a cab and gave her address to the driver. Then she sat back in the seat and the tears began to flow.

"What now" Beth asked.

"Get through the night, work a full day tomorrow and then go home."

"Go home and do what?"

"I don't honestly know. Being an outraged husband is not an option. I'm not a hypocrite and I can't very well rage at her considering what I've been doing. I will try and find out why she cut me off, started ignoring me and then took up with your husband. For all I know he isn't the first. I may try and find out who and how many."

"Is there a divorce in your future?"

"It is possible, very possible."

"I think you will be happier in one of the guest bedrooms tonight sweetie. I'd love to have you in my bed tonight, but I don't really think that all of you would be there."

"You are probably right."

I slept fitfully, which is to say I got almost no sleep at all. I could not for the life of me understand what had happened to Jennie. What had I done for her to do to me what she did?

Three cups of coffee didn't do much to start the day off and as I waited for Beth I saw that she hadn't wasted any time in getting started on Frank. It was only seven in the morning and a van with Acoma Locks painted on the side was pulling into the circular drive up front.

On the way to work Beth asked me if I had given any more thought to whether I was going for a divorce or not.

"That's the second time you have asked me that. Why?"

"Because your alimony will be based on what you make. I can hold off on that raise I am going to give you until after the divorce is final and that way you won't get hosed so bad."

"Thanks for the thought, but a raise to regional managers pay isn't going to be all that significant."

"Maybe not a regional manager's pay, but that's not what I intend to give you. You won't take a promotion to vice president, but you are going to get a vice president's salary and benefits. You saved my company sweetie. You can "Aw shucks, it wasn't really me" all you want, but it wouldn't have happened without you and you know it. It all happened because you - you Martin - you said you would help me with my Angela problem. Everything that happened resulted from your agreement to help me, and you will never convince me otherwise, so don't even try."

"Yes, ma'am."

"There, that wasn't so hard, was it?"

It was a long day at work and I wasn't sure I even earned my pay as my mind was elsewhere. It was on my life and where it was going. On Jennie and what had happened between us. On what I had done to make the change in her. How had she gone from a missionary only prude to having an affair or affairs? Who had been the one who caused her to do something about her appearance? Who? Why? I wanted to know. I needed to know. Jennie had called twice that day and I told her that I wouldn't talk to her until I came home that night to pack. She had cried, "Pack?!! Oh God, no Martin, ple..." and I hung up on her.

The answers to the questions that I had to have answered were at the house, but by the end of the day I had to force myself to go home to get them.

<<O>>

She had screwed up and she knew it. She had no one else but herself to blame and she knew that also, but she loved Martin and she didn't not want to live without him in her life. How could she save anything out of the mess she had made? Her only hope was that he would listen to her as she tried to explain what had led her to do what she had done, believe her when she told him how much she loved him and that he would give her the forgiveness she would beg for.

The one thing she did know was that she had to be completely honest with him. She would not sugar coat the pill on what she had done with Frank. She would not tell Martin that she was just having dinner with a friend. No, Martin would get it all, no matter how bad it made her look. She owed the man she loved that much, at least.

She knew that the mood when Martin came home was not going to be good so she didn't bother with making dinner. There would be no sitting down, eating in silence and then going:

"Okay, what would you like to talk about?"

If she wanted to keep Martin she was going to have to do something to blunt the anger he would be bringing home with him. She would have to distract him long enough to give her time to get it all out before he went on the attack. She thought long and hard on it and finally decided the best thing to do would be to do the last thing he would expect.

She was sitting where she could see him when he pulled into the drive. She was as ready as she could be. She took a deep breath and prayed that it would work and that she could get Martin back before she lost him.

I still had no idea of how I was going to handle it when I opened the door and walked into the house. I stopped in my tracks at the sight that greeted me. Jennie stood there in a sheer black teddy and 'Come Fuck Me' pumps with four inch heels and holding a filled martini glass out to me. Dumbfounded, I reached out and took it from her hand.

"Would you like your blowjob before my explanation or after?"

My mind wasn't working. This wasn't my Jennie. I stood there holding the martini as she said:

"I'll take that to mean you want it first" and she knelt down in front of me, pulled down my zipper and had a hand on my cock before I got myself together enough to say:

"Damn it Jennie, this is no…" and that was as far as I got before her hot mouth enveloped me. "Oh shit" I thought as I felt her tongue work on me, "It is the only blow job I will ever get from her so I might as well enjoy it." I looked down to see her looking up at me as her head moved back and forth on my cock. I saw her hands undoing my belt and my trousers fell to the floor. She took her mouth off of me long enough to pull my briefs down and then her mouth captured me again.

With my briefs out of the way her left hand fondled my nuts and I moaned as she took my cock all the way to the back of her throat. Her right hand went to my ass and she teased my butt hole with a finger and I groaned as the cum rushed out of me and into her mouth. She didn't pull back. Both of her hands gripped my ass and she held me as she swallowed my discharge and then she held me in her mouth until I became limp. She stood up, took the martini from my hand and took a sip and then handed the glass back to me.

"I want very much to kiss you right now Martin, but given what I just did, I don't want to gross you out. You might not like the taste of yourself."

"What the hell is this all about Jennie?"

"I wanted to relax you Martin. I wanted to relax you enough that you will sit down and give me a chance to save my marriage. I heard you introduce me to your boss last night as your "about to be ex-wife" and I want to change your mind if I can."

"Why the hell do you want to save our marriage Jennie? You have spent the last couple of years not showing any interest in me whatever. Why, after I find out about you having other men in your life, are you suddenly so interested in keeping me?"

She knelt down in front of me again and said, "Step out of your pants Martin" and then she pulled the out of the way as I lifted my feet. As she stood up, she stuck her tongue out and licked my cock and it twitched. It wanted her mouth again.

"Take a sip of your martini Martin and come sit down and I'll tell you everything."

I followed her into the family room and sat down on the couch. She took the easy chair across from me and said:

"I want to save our marriage Martin because I love you. I have never loved anyone but you and I want to stay with you."

"What about Frank?"

"Frank was a mistake Martin, a stupid mistake made by a stupid woman who was upset because her husband ignored her and wouldn't have anything to do with her. A woman who thought her husband didn't want her any more. I was vulnerable; Frank saw it and he took advantage of the situation. I could have said no, but I didn't."

"Why would you think I didn't want you anymore?"

"When was the last time you made love to me Martin?"

"I don't remember."

"Exactly my point Martin. Oh, I know why you lost interest in me. I know that I didn't look all that appealing and even when we made love I was a prude. Making love felt nice, but it wasn't all that big a thing to me. It was something that I could take or leave and as I let myself go you didn't push for sex and since I was so-so on the subject anyway I said nothing and things slid away from us.

"It wasn't until I joined that book discussion group at the library and was befriended by Alice and the others that things changed for me."

I sat there and listened as she told the story of the video tapes and how they made her want to try things with me, of looking in the mirror and suddenly realizing why I didn't bother her for sex anymore and how she set out to bring me back to her.

"I worked hard Martin, I busted my ass to make myself appealing to you, but you never noticed. You never commented on the change in me, not once. All you had time for was your job. Other men were looking at me, other men were making passes at me, but I couldn't even get you to acknowledge that there was a change in me. I got bitter Martin. I did all that work to make myself better for you, but you couldn't be bothered. I made up my mind that I had worked hard enough to get myself in shape for you, but I'd be damned if I was going to crawl to you and demand that you look at me. By God, you were going to have to come to me. I know now that it was stupid of me. If I had just forced the issue, we wouldn't be where we are now."

She told me how Alice had noticed her being out of sorts and how she had told Alice everything and how Alice had come up with the phone numbers plan. She told me of the night at the bar and how she had gloried in the attention she got.

"They wanted me Martin; every one of them wanted me, but you didn't. I was primed and ready Martin. The tapes had set me on the path to wanting to give you the love life you deserved, but you didn't seem to want me. You just didn't seem to care about me at all. I'm not blaming all the drinks I had that night, although they probably had something to do with lowering my inhibitions, but I was primed and ready to be fucked Martin and I let my good sense get away from me and Frank was there to pounce.

"I knew it was stupid and when I got home, I was sorry as hell that I'd done it. The next morning I made up my mind to force the issue and while you were eating breakfast, I took a quick shower and then hurried naked back to the kitchen, but you had already gone. Last night I was going to meet you at the door the way I did tonight, but then you called and said you were going out of town again. I asked you to come home and I told you that I needed you and you pushed me away again. Five minutes after you hung up, Frank called and I thought, "At least someone wants me" and I agreed to have dinner with him knowing that we would probably end up in a motel. We went to the restaurant and the rest you know."

"Why would you go to a motel since you knew I wouldn't be coming home?"

"Your house and your bed Martin. I couldn't do it here, I just couldn't."

"So you are saying that this is all my fault? That I caused you to do fuck another man?"

"No, that isn't what I'm saying. I accept that I'm responsible for what I did. What I'm doing is explaining how it happened and I'm hoping you will understand why it happened. I made a monumentally stupid mistake and I'm begging you to forgive me. Please Martin I love you, God knows I do, and I hope you do too. Just give me a chance to prove it Martin. That is all I'm asking for, your forgiveness and a chance."

I stared at her and thought about our situation. I had thought she was disinterested when what she was doing was waiting for me to say, "Wow, what have you done to yourself." I had noticed the changes and thought they were for someone else. Talk about two people lacking in communication skills. And what about what I had been doing. A pot calling the kettle black situation if there ever was one.

I loved her; I had always loved her, even when she had seemed disinterested. Should I tell her what I had been doing? Show her that we were even? No, I didn't think so. It might not make things better and in fact, it could make things worse. I wanted to give her what she wanted, the forgiveness she was asking for, but first, I had to know.

"Was Frank the only one or were there others?"

"There was no one else Martin, no one!"

"And Frank got all the benefit of your newfound sexuality?"

She blushed and then she said, "No, not all of it. He got my first blow job and it was a pretty poor one since it was my first, but I learned from it though and the one you just got was a lot better. And he did get me into some positions other than missionary. He wanted all of it, but I did save one thing just for you."

"What?"

"He wanted my ass Martin, but I told him the only one who would ever go there would be you."

<<O>>

She looked at him, unable to read what he was thinking by looking at his face. She had deliberately lied in indicating that she and Frank had only done it the one time. She felt hat was a confession enough. It wouldn't help the matter if Martin will know of the other times. He didn't need to know how far she had gone on those times and he sure didn't need to know that some of it was in his house and on his bed.

Let him believe he would be the first on most of it. If he stayed she would make it up to him. She promised herself if he stayed he would never regret it, not for one second. She had painted herself as a cheat and she knew she had shocked him by being as forward as she had been, but she didn't know if it had worked. "Please God," she prayed, "Let him forgive me."

<<O>>

"Hey girlfriend, how are you doing?" Alice asked.

"Not bad," Jennie said, "I'm hanging in there."

"The reason I'm calling is to let you know that Tina won't be playing cards with us tonight. She's coming down with something. She thinks it's the flu. I've lined up a sub for her though. We still on for seven?"

"Yes."

"What's the matter? You sound a little down."

"Every once in a while it catches up with me. The things that happened and the way things went."

"Buck up girlfriend, you'll survive. See you tonight."

She put down the phone and got busy cleaning the place up and preparing the refreshments. The doorbell rang at six forty-five and she answered it to find Alice and another woman standing there. The woman looked familiar and it took her a second or two to recognize her.

"Oh my God, it's you, it really is you."

"Surprise, surprise," Alice said. "Norma, meet Jennie. Jennie, meet Norma, also known to us as Angel Dust. She is in town to visit family and I asked her to fill in for Tina."

"Well, come on in. Don't just stand there, come in, come in. Honey, come here a minute."

"What" asked Martin as he walked into the room.

"Honey, I would like you to meet Norma. Norma, this is my husband Martin and next to me, he is one of your biggest fans."

"I am?"

"You sure are. You watch her at least once a week."

"I do?"

Alice laughed and said, "Try and imagine her without her clothes on."

He stared at Norma and suddenly the light bulb went on over his head and he stepped forward and extended his hand as said:

"Welcome to our humble abode."

Jennie took Norma's hand and said, "Follow me into the kitchen and while I'm making you a drink I'll tell you how you almost ruined my marriage and then saved it."

As Jennie led Norma away, Alice asked, "What was that all about? What did I miss?"

"Long story, but you will have to get it from Jennie."

"You two seem to be getting along fine."

"We are. By the way, I never have thanked you for trying to help. Even though Jennie never did get to use the phone number ploy you did try to help and I appreciate it."

"Hey, what are friends for? So, how does it feel knowing that you are going to be a daddy?"

"It still hasn't caught up to me yet. Come on. Let's get the other two and play some Euchre."

The End

Here is a sample from another story you may enjoy:

Just Plain Bob

Just A Back-up Guy

TABOO ROMANCE

I looked down at the legal pad on the desk and rolled the pen between my fingers as I tried to organize the words in my mind. It would have been much easier for me if I was in front of a computer. When at the computer, my thoughts seemed to flow right to my fingers and the words would quickly appear on the screen. Hit 'print' and it would be done. Neat, single spaced lines of 11 point Times New Roman that would say it all, but to me that would be too impersonal. I needed for this to be personal; I needed what I was going to say to be an expression of "me", and so I would do it in my own handwriting. As one part of my brain tried to organize what I was going to say, another part was busy remembering what it was that led to my need to say it.

I had known Grace since the fourth grade. She moved in two doors down from me and we were the same age, so we ended up in the same class at school. Even at nine, there was something about Grace that pulled me to her. At that age, most boys were still thinking of girls as "yucky", but I never felt that way about Grace.

We didn't see much of each other when we weren't in school. She was busy playing with dolls with her girlfriends while me and the other guys my age were playing "cops and robbers" or "cowboys and Indians" or sandlot baseball. It wasn't until I was twelve that I started noticing girls and Grace was the one I seemed to notice most of all.

It was the eighth grade when things changed. Our school wasn't all that big and the boys and girls had to share the gym for the physical education period. Usually the guys would have the gym one day while the girls would have the swimming pool and vice versa.

It was the boy's day for the gym, but when we got there, the gym teachers had a surprise for us. The boys and girls were going to share the gym that day. They were going to teach us to dance! Boys and girls were paired up. A record started playing and they were teaching us the waltz. I was paired up with Susan Jaffery and Grace was paired up with Dale Harding. I didn't know why, but I got upset watching Grace dancing with Dale. At the end of the period, it was announced that for the rest of the school term, the boys would have the gym on Mondays and Thursdays and the girls would have it Tuesdays and Fridays. Wednesdays would be dance class and that we would keep the same partners. That news upset me a lot. Not that dance class was bothering me, but that I was stuck with Susan and Dale with have Grace.

And that was the start of it. Dale had Grace and Dale kept Grace from then on. The two of them were inseparable. By the tenth grade, I was eating my heart out over Grace. What made things really bad for me was that Grace, probably unwittingly, led me on. Dale's parents were both teachers, and they always traveled on summer vacations, which usually lasted for two and a half to three months. While Dale was gone, Grace asked me to take her to a party that Dale was supposed to have taken her to. We had a good time and when I asked her for a date she said yes. I dated her for the entire time that Dale was gone. She was receptive to my kisses and our necking got pretty hot and heavy at times. After two months, I asked her to go steady with me and she said, "Oh come on, Rob. You know I'm Dale's girl."

That didn't stop her from necking with me, though, and she kept dating me until Dale got back from vacation.

Three months into the 11th grade, Dale and Grace got into an argument (over something or other) and they broke up. Grace asked me if I would be her escort to a couple of parties she wanted to go to over the holidays and I, of course, said yes. We dated right up to Christmas when one night, I was about to pick her up at her house and take her to a party when her mother answered the door.

"Grace isn't here, Rob. She left with Dale about half an hour ago."

I went to the party alone. When I got there, I saw Grace and Dale dancing. I went up to them to tap Dale on the shoulder so I could cut in, but he turned and told me to go away.

"Not until Grace and I talk."

"She's not going to talk to you so beat it."

"Okay. I wanted to do this quietly and not make a scene, but if a scene is what you want, then a scene is what you'll get." I turned to Grace and said loud enough for everyone to hear, "Would it have killed you to call me and break our date instead of letting me show up at your front door and have your mother tell me that you had already gone?"

Grace looked away from me while Dale pushed me and said, "Get the fuck out of here, Rob."

"Keep your hands to yourself, Dale."

"Oh yeah? What are you going to do about it?" and he shoved me again.

"This," I said as I hit him as hard as I could. It broke his nose and blood sprayed all over Grace's green dress as he went to his knees. "Hey, red and green" I said as I pointed at Grace's dress. "Very Christmassy." And I turned and left the party.

Grace called me around noon the next day. "How could you embarrass me like that? And my dress is ruined! I can't get the blood stains out."

"Your own fault, Grace. What did you think was going to happen when what you did was leave me standing on your front porch? You think I was going to worry about how you felt when you couldn't have cared less about how I was going to feel when I rang your doorbell and you weren't there? Thanks for calling, Grace," and I hung up on her.

About three weeks into the spring term, I came out of Burger Heaven, where I had a part-time job, and found Dale waiting for me by my car. He had eight or nine people with him, including Grace, and a few other girls. As I walked up to my car, Dale said, "You and I have some business to settle. You sucker punched me that ni…" and I hit him. He wasn't expecting it. I guess he thought I'd just stand there and listen to him spout off until he decided to swing, but I wasn't having any of it. I stepped up and hit him again and broke his recently reset nose again. His hands flew up to his face and that left him wide open, so I hit him three more times and was going for more when I was pulled away from him.

"A sucker punch is a blow targeted on your blindside when you least expect it. I was facing you at the party, and after pushing me the second time, you should have expected me to do something. You came here tonight looking for a fight, so you should have been expecting it tonight, too. Stay away from me, Dale. Your nose can only be broken so many times before it starts looking like a pancake in the middle of your face."

I looked over at Grace, but she looked away. I got in my car and drove on home. Dale did stay out of my way from then on and eventually Grace stopped looking away whenever I glanced her way.

If you enjoyed this sample, look for **Just A Back-up Guy**.

Also by this Author:

From the Author

If you enjoyed any of my books then please share the love and promote my books in Amazon.

If you write me a review and send me an email I will send you a free book, or many.
(Just know that these emails are filtered by my publisher.)

Good news is always welcome.

One Last Thing, For Kindle Readers...

When you turn the page, Kindle will give you the opportunity to rate this book and share your thoughts on Facebook and Twitter. If you enjoyed my writings, would you please take a few seconds to let your friends know about it? Because... when they enjoy they will be grateful to you and so will I.

Thank You!

An Open Letter from Just Plain Bob

A message for those who like my stories, those who hate my stories, those who are indifferent and those who have yet to make up their minds.

I have often stated that I really don't care what others think about my stories, that I write for my own enjoyment and then I offer to share. If you like my stories fine and if you don't, also fine since I have already satisfied my target audience - me!

It is human nature to strive to get better. If you take up bowling your first games are going low scoring, but you will work and practice to get better and as your average climbs you may forget the game where you had three gutter balls and shot an eighty-six, but that game is still there in your past.

Your first time on the golf course you shot an eighty on the front nine, but did you settle for that being your game or did you work to improve? You may eventually get a three handicap, but that nine hole eighty is still there as part of your past.

When you hired in at your job did you say, "Cool, I got it made" and do nothing more than what you barely had to do or did you go to work thinking that, "Someday I'm going to be running this place." You might never climb that high, but human nature says that you are going to at least try.

It is the same with authors who write stories and post them on sites like Literotica. Their first stories might not be all that good, but comments and feedback along with a desire to get better drive them toward putting out a better product or to at least try.

I'm no different. My first stories might not have been all that great, but they are still there on the hard drive. I like cheating wife stories and five years ago I found my first adult site that catered to cheating wife stories. It was a pay site, but it had a policy of giving a free lifetime membership to anyone who submitted five stories to the site. How hard can that be I said to myself as I sat down and fired up the word processor and went to work.

I sent my five stories in and sat back to enjoy my free membership and a funny thing happened. I started getting feedback, most of it positive, and I became hooked. I started cranking out more stories. The site I was sending my stories to had seven categories:

Bisexual
Cream Pie

Groups
I Watch
Gang Bang
Racial
SM/BD

I know nothing about bisexual or SM/BD and I had no interest in Groups so all the stories I wrote I tailored for the four remaining categories:

Cream Pie
I Watch
Gang Bang
Racial.

I turned out eight stories a month, two for each category, which means that after five years I have over 120 stories in each of those categories and they are all still on the hard drive.

A year ago I received an email asking me why I never posted stories on Literotica. The answer? I didn't know about Lit. I pulled it up, liked what I saw, and started sending in stories to it. All new stories? No, not hardly, not with over 400 stories sitting on the hard drive. Maybe one new story for each fifteen or so old ones. The newer ones are better, at least I think they are and I have received some feedback that leads me to believe that others think so too, and I will continue to write new ones.

But I am still going to recycle what is on the hard drive, stories that were written specifically to fit the four categories. That means that those of you who hate cream pie stories still have eighty or so to look forward to. Ditto for those who call me a racist; you will get another seventy or so interracial stories.

Those who hate wimps will only see about fifty more of those because the stories I sent to the I Watch category were split 50/50 between what some call wimps and some call "real men." Why the 50/50 split? It came from listening to the readers. I would get feedback asking me why all the men in my stories were hard asses. "In real life men are more forgiving, especially if it is the first indiscretion." So I would write stories with forgiving husbands and boyfriends and then the next batch of feedback would say, "Why are all your husbands spineless wimps" and I'd write stories that went back the other way.

Eventually I came to realize that I was wasting my time - there was no way I could write a story that would satisfy everybody and that is when I adopted my philosophy of writing for my own enjoyment and then offering to share.

As far as the gangbang stories? Well, what can I say? Gangbangs are gangbangs and there are still eighty or so of them to go.

The bottom line is that Literotica readers are going to see more of my old stories than my new ones. If I'm still around three or four years from now it will probably go the other way, more new than old.

I feel the need to respond to some of the comments and emails I have received. By far the largest percentage comes from people who say, "You are an asshole because all women are not whores and sluts and that's all you make them out to be."

Next most common is, "You must really hate women you sick fuck."

"You must be a wimp because all the men in your stories are wimps" is up there in the top ten along with, "Why don't you give it a rest and go crawl off in a hole somewhere."

There is a lot more, but I'm only going to address those four and in reverse order.

I won't stop and go crawl in a hole because I am enjoying the hell out of what I am doing and remember what I said, I am doing this for MY OWN ENJOYMENT and then I offer to share. Some obviously like my sharing with them and so I will continue to do so. No one is holding a gun to a reader's head and telling them they must click on a Just Plain Bob story or die. It is a conscious choice on the reader's part to move that mouse and click on that story.

When a man finds out he has a cheating wife or girlfriend there are only a limited number of ways he can handle it. If he loves her he can forgive, try to forget and try to hold on and somehow make things work. He can turn his back on her, walk away and get on with his life. The third option is to take revenge.

According to a good portion of those who send me feedback the first and second options are proof that the men are wimps. If the man takes the third option he is still considered a wimp if he doesn't do some sort of physical damage to the woman and her lover. These readers believe that the only way not to be a wimp is to kill, maim and destroy everything in sight. Doing that however, will invariably get the man throw in jail and that is why it so rarely happens in real life.

In real life most revenge takes place in the man's head when he says to himself, "I should have _____ (fill in the blank) the fucking cunt!" I know this because I have been there and done that (see The Dark Trilogy). In my stories I try to mirror real life so kill, maim and destroy are going to be for the most part absent. Outside of some fisticuffs there will be very little physical violence in my stories. Most of my husbands are going to do what I did, what several of my friends and others that I know have done, forgive, or walk away. If this makes them wimps and me a wimp for writing the story that way, so be it.

Next is the "I must hate all women." Nothing could be farther from the truth. I love women. I lust after women. I even like whores and sluts. I have been married four times, engaged two other times (that did not end in marriage) and I have always had girlfriends between marriages. My philosophy is that women were put on this earth for me to enjoy and I'm not talking just sexually. I could sit at the mall (and have) for hours and just girl watch.

The engagements, girlfriends and three of the four marriages bring me to the #1 anti JPB comment on the list.

"You are an asshole because all women aren't whores and sluts."

Well dear reader, you can not prove that by me! I will say up front that I KNOW all women aren't whores and sluts, BUT the majority of the women in my life were. My mother ran around on my father for years while he was driving a truck for a living. My Aunt Margaret cheated regularly on my Uncle Bill, as did my Aunt Mildred on my Uncle Paul. My Aunt Betty fucked around on my Uncle Bob for years and finally left him for his brother, my Uncle Wendell. Uncle Wendell in turn caught her on her knees at his company Christmas party giving Season's Greetings to his boss.

My sister is three times divorced and each divorce came about when the then current husband caught her out spreading pollen. Both of the engagements I mentioned ended when I found out that I was not the one and only and a lot of the girls I dated between marriages never made it to engagement status for the same reason.

And that brings me to my three ex-wives. The first one, Helen (I believe I commented on her in the intro to The Dark Trilogy) had seven different lovers before I found out what was going on. I was living proof that love is blind. Ditto with my second wife. She had a secret life that she hid from me and when I found out about her brother, his friends and the gangbangs she was history.

My third marriage ended in divorce because of a different kind of cheating (and I can just imagine the outrage I am going to get over this) - she cheated on me with an idea. I was away from home on business, she was lonely, a couple of Jehovah's Witnesses knocked on the door and my wife, with nothing better to do invited them in. When I came home from my trip I found out that she had found God. On a scale that runs from TRUE BELIEVER on one end to ATHEIST on the other you will find me just to the right of AGNOSTIC and since I would not allow myself to be SAVED the marriage eventually died.

So yes, I write about sluts and whores because as everyone knows, you tend to write about the things you know. And I do like sluts and whores, just not the ones that lie to me and cheat on me.

So be forewarned - if you click on a Just Plain Bob story you will be getting sluts, whores and husbands who do not kill, maim and destroy. There are other things you will rarely find in a Just Plain Bob story. Even though I try to mirror real life my stories all take place in StoryLand. In StoryLand STDs and un-wanted pregnancies do not exist unless the author feels like they may add something to the story. Bad things do not happen in StoryLand unless the author so wills it and no amount of "You should have…" in comments and feedback will change a story already posted.

Lastly, I will touch on a truth. None of what I have written here means shit because the same readers will still read the same stories that they profess to hate and make the same comments they have always made. Knowing this, I will deliberately post stories that will have them frothing at the mouth.

It is the least I can do for an adoring public.

Thank you!

Just Plain Bob
justplainbob@awesomeauthors.org

www.ingramcontent.com/pod-product-compliance
Lightning Source LLC
Chambersburg PA
CBHW071416170626
46811CB00003B/1432